DESTINY
EXPRESS

DESTINY EXPRESS

A NOVEL BY

Howard A. Rodman

ATHENEUM New York 1990

Atheneum
Macmillan Publishing Company
866 Third Avenue, New York, N.Y. 10022
Collier Macmillan Canada, Inc.

Library of Congress Cataloging-in-Publication Data
Rodman, Howard.
    Destiny express : a novel / by Howard A. Rodman.
        p.   cm.
    ISBN 0-689-12090-7
    I. Title.
PS3568.034858D48 1990
813'.54—dc20   89-15166   CIP

        10 9 8 7 6 5 4 3 2 1
    Printed in the United States of America

To
my parents
and to
Joe Savago
(1948–1987)
"Thought of you as everything
I've had, but could not keep."

DESTINY
EXPRESS

O N E

ALONE IN THE CORRIDOR HE SCRAPED A WOOD
match against the wall, lighting up another cigarette. There
was a bare overhead bulb every meter or so along the low
unfinished ceiling, no other light. From within the screening room he heard sounds, low voices, but they were
unintelligible, and he could not tell just which scene was
being shown.

Lang's feet, like his hands, were quite large; and he
walked with an erect military carriage. He had been out
here for most of the film, extinguishing coarse imported
cigarettes on the floor, and watching the play of his distinctly multiple shadows. The shadows elongated and fore-
shortened as he paced the hallway. He had long since tired
of watching them. Lang adjusted his monocle, and idly lit
one more match.

Then he heard the explosion, found himself smiling
in recognition: asylum director Baum, under the hypnotic
possession of his most famous patient, the archfiend Mabuse,
had just blown up the chemical plant. It was one of his
favorite shots and one, he knew, which occurred quite
near the end. Lang walked down the corridor, knocked
sternly on the door to the projection booth.

"Pfeiffer?" he said, when there was no reply. He
became aware that his right upper wisdom tooth was

throbbing again, had been throbbing, really, for some time.

"I'm sorry, Herr Lang," came the voice from the other side of the door. He had walked to the end of the hall, halfway back, before it occurred to him that there was someone else in the projectionist's booth, someone he was meant not to see. Finding it at once too bright in the corridor, Lang worked the middle door, eased himself into the screening room, two rows behind the insipid Kosterlitz and his secretary, who constituted today's audience. He remembered that Thea had asked him to buy this month's *Die Dame*, which he could get Erich to pick up at the all-night newsstand just off Ku-damm. Lang would remember the magazine and Thea would be pleased and with any luck he could forestall one of the tedious arguments which had of late become their staple. Onscreen, Doctor Mabuse—who in his heyday had manipulated the run of cards at the casino, the flow of paper currency, perhaps the course of Fate itself—was instructing Baum, from beyond the grave.

"The belief of the normal citizen in the powers he has elected," the superimposed shade of Mabuse told the psychiatrist, "must be destroyed. And when everything has been shattered, on this we will build the realm of crime."

Just ahead, Kosterlitz put his head on his secretary's shoulder, a childlike gesture which Lang found oddly moving. Turning his head, he saw only the glare of the projector, flickering beams of light, given weight by cigarette smoke. He would have to ask Pfeiffer, later, who the mystery visitor had been. Hearing the high whine of automobiles at top speed, Lang leaned back to watch the final night chase of his latest film, *The Testament of Doctor Mabuse.*

He had seen it perhaps fifty times, and would be expected, as a courtesy, to sit through it some ten more, in the round of prerelease screenings before the March 23 premiere at UFA-Palast. "I wouldn't want," Kosterlitz had told him, in the library of Lang's club, the Explorers', "to see it without you." Kosterlitz had added: "Unless, of course, you're bored with it by now." Lang decided he would kill Kosterlitz one day, kill him brutally, for just that remark. The roar of car engines grew louder and seemed, somehow, to be in synchronization with his toothache. He would have to do something about it if the pain did not abate.

"After him!" Inspector Lohmann could be heard to insist. The Lohmann character, who had been quite a hit in Lang's previous film, *M*, had been imported here as Mabuse's nemesis. Lang would have preferred to use the hapless prosecutor von Wenk, of the original Mabuse film; but Bernhard Goetzke was not available to re-create the role, and Lang could not imagine the hapless prosecutor played by anyone else. Lang touched his monocle, a ribbonless, ingrowing affair which, rumor had it, could not be removed without recourse to surgery. Its convex outer surface glinted sullenly now in the white cinema light.

Blurred objects at the roadside, looming ghostlike in the headlights of Baum's car. Inspector Lohmann's car, moments behind, in pursuit.

Lang became aware of a rotten, tropical odor, perhaps one of the newer coal-tar derivatives. He placed a finger along a seam in the new carpet, brought the finger to his nose. Aniline cement. He was wondering how he could have been so stupid as to be thinking about having his driver Erich pick up the fashion magazine for Thea: Erich had called in sick, and Lang had taken the roadster. It was getting bad, he knew, if he could not recall which car he'd taken to drive to the studio. Now that he was aware of the coal-tar cement, he could not help but smell it, and think about the way his shoes would smell from having walked upon it. There was a meeting at six-thirty with Correll, UFA's head of production, which he could get out of. It might be best just not to show up. He had been quite cooperative with the courtesy screenings. Perhaps it was time, once more, to unleash the impulsive artiste.

Onscreen Rudolf Klein-Rogge, who played Mabuse, was hovering over poor Baum. Lang remembered the many takes they had done of the shot, because the camera dolly kept hitting some kind of a bump, and they'd had to lay down rails. Then Rudolf seemed unhappy, and missed his mark several times running. It took the better part of a fifteen-minute break to extract from Klein-Rogge just what had been bothering him.

"It's where I have to bend down," the actor said finally, in the voice a small child uses, imparting confidences to a trusted stuffed bear. "Here," he continued, pointing to his hairline, which had receded quite a bit in the ten years since Doctor Mabuse had made his debut.

"You have," Lang told him, "a heroic forehead, and should be proud."

"You can reshoot, with the head erect?"

"Of course," Lang had said, throwing his arm around the actor, squeezing the side of his neck.

4

"And you will not fool me now, by using one of the earlier takes?"

"Thea calls it your widow's peak," Lang said, guiding Klein-Rogge back to the lit portion of the set, avoiding cable underfoot. "It is part of what she finds attractive." Klein-Rogge had been the previous husband of Lang's wife, Thea. They'd been able to talk about it in the past year or so. Now, in the screening room, Lang could only wonder how the actor had put up with her, although, he told himself, Thea was younger then, and the kind of marriage she'd had with Klein-Rogge need not have been anything like the one she had with him. The tooth was making itself felt; and then Lang must have dozed off, because the next thing he knew the screen was alive, white leader with odd markings flashing bright and stroboscopic, loud cracklings, as the sound sputtered to a stop. Kosterlitz was already on his feet.

"You have surpassed yourself," Kosterlitz was saying.

"Coming from you—" Lang heard himself replying, as he rose and adjusted his trousers, which had bagged at the knees while he had been sitting.

"Quite fine," said Kosterlitz's secretary, a young woman with a flat, pleasant face Lang could not bring himself to regard with much seriousness.

"Thank you for coming." The pain had started up again. Trying the door, Lang found it locked from the outside. He pulled at the knob several times, somewhat frantically at first, then quite calmly, turning left and right, pulling and pushing, in all permutations. Beyond the door, he heard footsteps. Then the door opened outward and Lang, still holding the knob, had to perform a small dance to retain balance.

"Terrible mistake," said Pfeiffer, the projectionist.

"Eat shit," said Kosterlitz.

Lang shepherded Kosterlitz along the corridor, recalling *The Adventures of Fräulein Roland*, which Kosterlitz had written and directed, and through which Lang had been forced to sit two separate times. "Perhaps they merely wanted," Lang told him, "to assure a captive audience."

"No need. I was literally glued to my chair," said Kosterlitz, who was always using "literally" to mean "figuratively." Lang waited for him to single out for special praise just those scenes Lang himself hated most. (It had taken Lang ten viewings to be able to stand any of it.)

"The superimpositions were a poem," Kosterlitz went on. Lang had used them, hoping by visual clutter to camouflage the unlikeliness of a couple of turns of plot. Kosterlitz had been fooled, but Lang was not sure if that was saying much. It struck him that Pfeiffer's song and dance with the screening room door had been a delaying tactic, to allow the mystery man in the booth his unseen escape. Now the lower jaw seemed to be throbbing as well. It would have been far better to use the sound track to denote Baum's possession by the patient he'd intended to cure.

"Thank you, Herr Lang," the secretary was saying, as he held the door for her. Dusk was falling quickly. It was just after six P.M., on the last day of February.

"I can't tell you how glad it makes me," Lang heard himself saying, "that you were able to join us." They crunched gravel underfoot. "My best to Herr Freund," he added, recalling, somehow, the name of her fiancé.

"A poem," Kosterlitz repeated.

6

Fritz Lang was a tall man, with large features, who had celebrated his forty-second birthday almost three months previous. He'd been born and raised in Vienna, had blue eyes, and would have been, like his father Anton before him, an architect, had he not run away from home and school, to take up painting, in Paris and Zurich. Then the money ran out. Supporting himself as an illustrator of postcards—and occasionally as a cartoonist—Lang toured the Low Countries, Asia Minor, North Africa, China, Japan, and the South Seas. At twenty-four he landed back in Paris, resumed correspondence with his father, and with his mother, the former Paula Schlesinger. An exhibition of his Schiele-like paintings attracted some notice. On July 31, 1914, the socialist leader Jaurès was assassinated as he sat in the Café du Croissant; Lang, at a café two blocks away, decided it was time to get out, and took the last train to leave Paris before the outbreak of hostilities. He was taken prisoner in Belgium, but escaped across the border into Germany. Back in Vienna, he worked briefly as a joke-teller in a cabaret. Then he was conscripted. He fought on the Russian, Balkan, and Italian fronts, sustained several gunshot wounds, nearly lost his right eye. The last wound won him a year's convalescence in a Vienna hospital set aside for such things. The young lieutenant began writing stories, and took up the wearing of a monocle. He acted a bit, attracted the attention of Eric Pommer of the German Eclair film company, to whom he sold some stories. 1919: the telegram said, "Come to Berlin, to direct." His first film for Eclair-Bioscope, *The Weakling*, concerned a man destroyed by his love for a woman. In 1920 he met Thea von Harbou, a writer of popular stories and novels, who wore her hair short, and parted severely on one side. She was slightly his senior. They married two years later, each for the second time. She wrote the scenarios for all his films; and collaborating with her was nowhere near as difficult as he would have thought. She had blue eyes, paler than his own. When Lang's mother died, Thea stood with him at the funeral, and Anton confided to Lang the next day, over cups of chocolate, he thought his son had chosen well. It struck Lang as an odd thing for his father to be saying, at a time like that.

When they were still sleeping together, it was more likely Thea's bedroom than his own. Their first popular success, *Destiny*, in 1921, gave Lang a degree of power within the UFA studio. American rights were sold to Douglas Fairbanks, who remade it as *The Thief of Baghdad*, utilizing the same special effects, less well executed. The next year Thea wrote, and Lang directed, *Doctor Mabuse, the Gambler*, after the novel by Norbert Jacques. Lang chose Klein-Rogge for the title role. Thea had been afraid that he'd cast her ex-husband as a favor to her, as part of some more complex exchange; but he assured her this was not the case, Klein-Rogge was simply right for the part. *Mabuse* was termed "the reflexes of an epoch immortalized in celluloid"; "an excellent portrait of high society with its gambling passion and dancing madness, its hysteria and decadence, its expressionism and occultisms"; "a mirror of the age."

1923 was, looking back on it, the last year he'd been able to set aside any regular time for painting. Filming the *Nibelungen* saga, in two parts, was quite draining. He sailed to New York, awestruck by the way that city's skyline looked as the liner pulled into the harbor. He used the skyline as an inspiration for *Metropolis*, a tale from the city of the future, from one of Thea's novels. It cost more than any film ever made. Thousands of extras, sets of unparalleled size. Anton sent a letter, in labored copperplate, saying he'd seen it, and his son Fritz had turned out to be an architect, after all.

Lang's least favorite film, he'd have to say. Then Anton died. (It was said, among Vienna friends, he'd never been the same, after Paula.) The irony with which Lang wore the monocle, the military carriage, seemed to drop away after his father's death. No one said, as they did of the insipid Kosterlitz, that Lang was easy to work with. Early forties, that's not so old, Lang told himself now, between tooth spasms. He'd made four films since *Metropolis*, two for his own company, two for Seymour Nebenzal's Nero Films. There seemed no way around using UFA for distribution.

"Can I drop you?" Kosterlitz was asking. They had reached the point where the gravel path forked toward the parking lot, toward the office building.

"I have the Lancia," Lang replied, hearing it come out more arrogantly than he would have wished. He considered asking Kosterlitz's secretary to cancel the six-thirty meeting, decided instead to stand Correll up without notice. Lang looked back at the boxy, near-windowless concrete bunker, UFA's new administration building, which struck him less as architecture than as a set for a film about a movie studio. Even Anton would have designed something more felicitous. Lang found himself at his roadster. He wondered whether he'd said good-bye to Kosterlitz and the secretary, then decided he had. He sat down, adjusted the mirror to look at himself. It seemed to him that as he got older his ears got larger. Lang reset the mirror, started the machine, listened to the gravel kick up against the fender pan as he took off faster than really necessary. He made for UFA's diamond-lattice gates.

Lang drove the long way, through Nikolskoe, oaks and lindens all bare now, black branches holding up white frost, as if one had superimposed, just slightly off register, a photograph and its negative. Turning left at Glenicker, Lang thought to drive along the smaller roads for a while, before they widened at Wannseebrücke. It was just dark enough to try the headlights, not dark enough for them to be of much help. The overhead lamps at Potsdamer would be on, just the right light to shoot the nighttime car chase. But there were no other cars on the small roads now. To his left Lang sensed the water, dark and heavy, a few meters from the road. More a stillness than anything else. At once the blacktop rejoined Königstrasse, and Lang slid the Lancia adeptly into the stream of traffic. The newsstand at Zoo Station was fairly comprehensive, and would be more nearly on his way. He watched his shadow whip around as he passed the first large streetlamp. There was that little pastry shop in Schöneberg, which he always had trouble finding. He would set himself the task of driving past the pastry shop without stopping. If he could do that, perhaps the tooth would get better. It wouldn't work, he knew, unless he drove past quite slowly, near the curb, close enough to smell butter, and smell chocolate. Then the Zoo Station was upon him. He nosed the roadster into a vacant parking space. Lang sat in the car awhile, engine off, lighting a cigarette, obliterating shadow.

DESTINY EXPRESS

Lang was just past the entrance to the main waiting room when he heard his name; but there was no one he could think of, offhand, he really wanted to speak with just now. The waiting room's arched interior was lit by a huge overhead electrolier. Lang threaded his way along aisles of dark wood benches, toward the newsstand. He heard his name again, a woman's voice. He lengthened his stride, so as to outpace his pursuer without appearing to hurry.

"Fritz."

The voice was louder now, with less of a quizzical lilt, and he knew it would be hard to pretend, at this range, not to have heard. Lang turned around to see a woman, face painfully familiar, two leather-strapped suitcases and a third under her arm. Working his face in a show of recognition Lang spun right, to see Bert Brecht.

"Yes, darling, you're right," Brecht was saying.

"Bert, Helene," Lang said, pleased with the fact her name had come to him at the instant of need. She was an actress to whom he'd given a small part in *Metropolis*. Brecht smiled at him, and he supposed he was smiling back. Lang touched his monocle. Brecht, grinning, held a hand to his own wire-rims. It was more or less a standing joke between them. Track announcements echoed harsh and reverberant through the large arched space. It was not clear whether the people sitting on the benches were waiting for a train to be announced.

"They told us to be early," Helene was saying, "to check the trunks on through, but now we have forty-five minutes before they will even let us board."

"Why don't we take them," suggested Brecht, "to the baggage room?"

11

"I'll take them, please," said Lang.

"Check them for less than an hour?" Helene asked.

Brecht said, "Are we not, all of us, unclaimed luggage in the train station of history?"

"At least the large one," Lang insisted. He reached out, seized the handle, as she lifted her elbow to ease the bag's removal. Putting it at his feet, he noticed he and Brecht were wearing the same coat: brown leather, double-breasted, with a robe-style belt. It was the coat worn by Gus Grundgens, as the head of the criminals, in *M*. Brecht's seemed to be of sturdier leather. At once the track announcements ceased. The three looked at each other.

"Will you join me for a quick cup?" Lang asked finally.

"Train station coffee?" Brecht smiled again. Lang could smell his breath, which was foul.

"Are we not, all of us, consumers of train station coffee?" Lang asked, stepping back, lest Brecht decide to punch his bicep for the remark.

"Will we be able to hear the boarding announcements from the café?" asked Helene.

"Yes," Brecht said. "Yes."

He went off, busying himself with a cigar, leaving Lang and Helene to carry the luggage. She was wearing a cloche hat, of the type Thea would dismiss with a pointed remark. Lang could not imagine his wife and Frau Brecht getting along.

"Where are you going?" Lang inquired of Helene, as they walked.

"Prague."

"Vacation?" he said absently.

"For good," Helene told him. Lang became aware that something serious was going on here, but did not know quite how to ask. He made a vow to disregard the tooth, which was, he had to admit, relatively quiescent now, to disregard thoughts of Thea, that he might give fuller regard to what Helene was saying.

"When," Lang said finally, pitching his voice over the blare of track announcements, and finding it too loud when they suddenly ceased, "did you decide?"

"Perhaps three months," she said, looking at him directly for the first time. "But really just this morning, in terms of tickets and things."

"Three months," he found himself repeating. The tooth was throbbing, and he felt his attention lapse. It was a physical thing, really. Not at all a question of will, or concentration. More like a wave, slipping out to sea. Not a wave, but something like that.

"We know what they're going to make of the fire at the Reichstag," she was saying. Lang had read, in the morning paper, of the fire, and of the Dutch Communist whom the Nazis claimed had set it. He had imaged it as looking much like the conflagration he'd staged at the chemical factory, for the climax of *Testament*. When he'd read the newspaper he'd told himself the fire was something he would have to think about, and he'd made a note to buy the evening papers, to see what kind of attention he would have to pay.

"Bert's found us a table," Helene said. They were in the arcade now, huge sheets of angled glass suspended on a grid of ironwork trellises, many meters above, scarcely visible now, with no light from outside. The odor of wet wool and diesel fuel. Seated now, at a table in the semienclosed café, it came to Lang that he was in Zoo Station, to buy a fashion magazine for his wife, with a couple about to leave Germany, most likely for good, a decision they had made only within the day.

Brecht was reading an evening tabloid, half-aloud. Lang recalled meeting him at Piscator's, four years ago now, and soon after at a meeting of progressives someone had dragged him to. It seemed, briefly, that Lang would film Brecht's *Threepenny Opera*, but the financing had fallen through, and other projects intervened, and the film was finally made by Pabst. The two had met about *Threepenny* a few times, before the bottom had fallen out, and Lang recalled those times now with some fondness. Brecht hated film, and wrote only on onionskin paper, folded in half. Lang had told him that there was nothing in *Threepenny* that François Villon hadn't done five hundred years before. Now, in the train station café, they were exchanging good-byes. Lang tried to think about all this without resorting to notions of crossing paths, or the twinings of fate, which he'd relied on heavily in his thirties, but which he felt no longer as useful as they'd once been, and not becoming to a man of his maturity.

"Café au lait," Helene told the waiter.

Brecht held up two fingers. "A kirchetorte, as well."

"And a chocolate," Lang said. He had arrived late at the meeting of progressives, an overdecorated drawing room in Wilmersdorf, and got the impression Brecht had just been criticized for some sort of attitude problem. He'd caught, as he found a chair, the tail end of an autocritique on Brecht's part, in which Brecht promised to "work" on his hostility toward discipline. "I will recognize," Brecht had said, removing his wire-rims for emphasis, "necessity." It was a good line, with the right proportions of assertiveness and self-deprecation. Lang had made a note to remember it, for use with Correll, Kallmann, the others at UFA.

"Did you call Willi?" Helene was asking her husband.

"I'll drop him a letter." Brecht had removed his overcoat, and was wearing a gray tweed jacket of bulky cut, and a tieless blue shirt, buttoned to the neck. The height of the glass roofing created a confusion within Lang as to whether he felt "indoors." The waiter arrived, placing the chocolate in front of Lang, without having to ask.

"We've plenty of time," Brecht said, placing his cigar in the ashtray without extinguishing it. Helene blew once more at the surface of her coffee.

"Is there anything I can do," Lang asked, lighting a cigarette, summoning attentiveness, "in terms of errands, loose ends—"

"My comrades," Brecht replied suddenly, "will provide."

"It's not been easy," said Helene, in a tone of habitual apology.

"Thanks anyway," said Brecht finally.

"I have friends in Prague—" Lang began.

"As do we," Brecht said.

Helene, stirring her coffee, and bringing it to her lips one spoonful at a time, said nothing. Lang watched Brecht dump an unconscionable amount of sugar into the cup in front of him. Replacing the chrome-lidded bowl, Brecht lifted his arm, and Lang was reminded just how bad the man could smell. Lang's own chocolate was bitter, of the kind which required sweetening; but he found himself making no move toward the sugar.

Now Brecht was reading audibly from the paper in front of him: " 'Decree of February 28. Restrictions on personal liberty, freedom of speech and of the press, of association and assembly, as well as interference with the secrecy of the postal, telegraph and telephone service, and also confiscation of property—' You should pay attention, my friend. '—and the right to search private houses are permissible beyond the limitations placed upon them in law.' "

A luggage cart, piled with several trunks and cases, rolled toward them at medium speed, seemingly without human propulsion. The cart stopped at the grillwork which separated the café from the rest of the arcade. With great deliberation a boy of about ten years rose from behind a streamer trunk. He said, "Papa," working with some force to repress a smile, lest he be caught laughing.

Brecht said, "Stefan."

The boy at once disappeared, and the cart recommenced its mysterious rolling. "He'll be back," Brecht told Helene.

"They said we could board," Helene was saying, "as soon as they made up the sleepers. We're not in a sleeper. Our car is ready now. But not the sleepers."

"Mankind," Brecht said, placing a hand on his wife's forearm, "has been waiting centuries for a truly human history to commence. Compared with that epic patience—"

"My husband," Helene said without emphasis.

Lang saw, out of the corner of his eye, a figure which registered, but he could not decide, until some moments later, why his attention had been caught. The figure had the gait of Erich, his butler and driver, who'd stayed home, he'd said, with a terrible influenza. Either it had not been Erich, or Lang had been lied to about the illness. "I regret that you're leaving," Lang said, and was immediately sorry, because it did not speak to anything, and was something only a distracted man would say.

"Needless to say, we're full of regret, too." It was difficult to read, in Brecht's voice, the degree of irony. Lang had always found Brecht's deadpan difficult to deal with, but had put up with it; preferred it, in fact, to the painful earnestness of those legions with whom it was easy to work.

"I am particularly sorry," Brecht went on, again without much sign of how he wished to be taken, "that I shall miss Mabuse's last will." He spooned thick, syrupy dregs from the bottom of the cup. Lang wondered how he could stand it, without water, or something akin, to wash it down. "Yes. *The Testament of Doctor Mabuse.* Your film"—and here the italics were unmistakable—"with *politics.*"

"My film with politics."

"You think of politics," he said to Lang, making overscale gestures with his hands, as if playing to the back of the hall, "like something to be added, as sugar to coffee."

"You would know."

There were no track announcements. Lang listened to the continuous echo of footsteps, the distant hiss of escaping steam, poignantly unintelligible trackside farewells. Then his chocolate was cold.

"Can you see the clock from here?" Helene asked. The monocle was irritating his eye, and Lang removed it. He stubbed out his cigarette as well. It was a Boyard, black tobacco loosely packed in yellow corn paper. When they were unavailable, Lang smoked Gitanes, which had a similar tang, but were not as thick.

"Shut up," Brecht told his wife.

Stefan appeared, burrowing his head into Brecht's armpit from behind, until his father's arm was around his shoulders. He was smiling.

"You'll get a chance to see *Testament*, I'm sure, in Prague," said Lang. Standing, he caught the waiter by his forearm, gave him a large note. It occurred to Lang that he could have added, "or in Hollywood," but it was somewhat too late now, and thinking it over, he was glad he'd left it where it was. Then Brecht was looking at him, and he sat back down, tugging first at the knees of his trousers.

"The world is not sad," Brecht was saying. "The world is large."

Lang wondered why cigarettes tasted better after coffee than after chocolate. His whole jaw throbbed now. He told himself to be careful with heated liquids, or with iced ones for that matter. And told himself to remember, at the newsstand, to pick up all the papers, along with *Die Dame*, so he might get some sense of what was going on. Then came the announcement that the train to Prague, all points intermediate, was now accepting passengers.

Brecht looked at the kirchetorte, pristine save for a small triangle Helene had shaved from the tip, and offered it to Stefan. "Pity one can't eat," Brecht said, "as much as one wants to puke."

Lang kissed Helene on both cheeks, then, a bit foolishly, embraced her husband.

"To our work," Brecht said. The leather coats squeaked against one another.

"Oh yes," Lang said into his ear.

"We've lost," Brecht said, as if quoting.

He watched them work their way toward trackside, Stefan parting the crowd, Helene half a stride behind, bearing luggage.

At the newsstand, he bought a *Tageblatt*, the liberal Jewish paper, and the *Vössische Zeitung*, the good gray "Auntie Vöss." He asked for *Rote Fahne*, the Communist paper, and was told it had not appeared since the raid on Karl Liebknecht House, the party headquarters, on Friday. From time to time Lang used to look at the National Socialist paper, the *Beobachter*, but had decided, quite some time ago, not to purchase the damn thing. Hugenberg, who owned UFA, owned several newspapers as well, which were distributed free at the studio, and which Lang never read. He knew what they would say before he read them. It was his problem with most things. There was a painting, on the cover of *Die Dame*, of Marlene Dietrich, in broad watercolor strokes. He would like to meet Dietrich someday. Strangely, he never had.

The car was where he'd left it. He got in, lit a Boyard. The match flare gave accent to his cheekbones, his chin, the deepening vertical lines by the side of his mouth. Then he flicked the match out and smoked most of the cigarette in the dark before starting the motor. A car swept by, briefly illuminating the side of his face, to which he paid some attention in the rearview mirror. At home, he would have to shave. Hugenberg was minister of agriculture and economics as well as leader of the Nationalist party. Perhaps Hugenberg could introduce him to Dietrich. Surely it would not be beyond his power.

Lang pulled the roadster out of the parking space,

onto Hardenbergstrasse. He lit another wooden match. Its glare reflected off the Lancia's windshield, obliterating, for a moment, the night outside. There was a physical sensation as his eyes stopped down so as not to be overcome with light. Shaking the match out, he felt his pupils dilate, accommodating the night, and saw once more the red tail reflectors of the car in front of him.

Thea and he had lived for years just outside Berlin, in what newspapers invariably referred to as "the wealthy suburb of Dahlem." Two years ago, finding the commute onerous and feeling, obscurely, that his life would be better were he closer to the center of things, he'd leased a pied-à-terre in a marble-fronted apartment building on Breitenbachplatz. Seven rooms, three fireplaces, a balcony from which Lang found himself continually tempted to deliver himself of a speech, inciting passersby. Over the past year or so the house in Dahlem—with her dachshunds, his pre-Columbian art—had become Thea's, the pied-à-terre his. He'd actually come to prefer it. You could leave your shoes outside the door, and they'd be polished in the morning, although he'd never caught sight of the mechanism by which this occurred. (At present the house was being redone, the dogs boarded; and Thea was staying at Breitenbachplatz. She'd move back to the house in a couple of weeks, and it would be, in many senses, a relief.)

It was too late for the pastry shop. There was a tobacconist, just across from the Sportpalast, who carried Boyards. Lang made two right turns. The Mercedes sedan just behind made two right turns as well. Back on Hauptstrasse, he thought he saw the same Mercedes, several cars back now, but could not be sure. He had three packs, which would be enough for a white night, if it came to that. He stopped abruptly, at the corner of Hochbannen, to avoid hitting a cyclist in cap and knickers. "I should have eaten something," he heard himself saying aloud.

The man at the desk handed him some shirts on hangers which Lang had left to be laundered two days previous. One of them, the white cotton voile, was a particular favorite.

"Thank you," he said to the deskman. When things had been bad, a few weeks back, he'd gotten into the habit of asking the deskman whether Frau Lang were at home, to spare himself the shock, at the door, when his home was empty. He had stopped asking when he was no longer sure he could keep his voice casual. Now he would ask, or not, with no particular freight attached, one way or the other.

Lang climbed two flights of stairs whose treads, just slightly too deep for his stride, he'd never gotten used to. The corridor walls were of a dark mahogany inlay, the carpet a tight burgundy weave, and it was a tribute to something that the hall smelled more of wood than of wool. Working the lock, entering, and flicking on the overhead, he saw a rose in the cut-glass vase on the foyer table, a shorthand they'd worked out back then, that he should not expect her home. Then he took off his shoes, left them outside the door, which he shut quietly, pleased with himself for remembering just how badly they needed shining. Lang placed *Die Dame*, together with the mail, on the foyer table, just touching the vase's octagonal base. He would go out for dinner, or perhaps not eat. Lang could not bear dining alone at his own table. Sometimes, when there was some bread he could slice, and veal, or a roast, he would make himself a sandwich and eat standing up. But he could not bring himself to do that tonight. He sat down in his favorite chair, the red leather one, stacking the packs of Boyards on the table adjacent for reassurance. It might just be possible to do something about the superimpositions Kosterlitz had liked so much. He would call Nebenzal, his producer, and find out if UFA had already made up the release prints.

Then an old weariness came over him, and he knew that he did not want to tinker with *Testament*; not at all. He got up, busied himself with gin, vermouth, cocktail shaker. The tooth was not bothering him as much as it might. He arranged kindling and logs in the fireplace. He would watch the fire, then go out, get something to eat. (If he went to sleep now, he knew he'd wake after four or five hours, then have to contend with the balance of the night. Far better to have a full stomach, not even attempt bed, until midnight.)

It occurred to him that he wanted to read a Karl May Western, but he remembered they were all at Dahlem, with the exception of one he'd brought to the Nero Films office on Friedrichstrasse, to lend to Nebenzal. Fire well ablaze, Lang settled down now with the newspapers. Thea had referred to her new companion only as "the American," and he supposed it serious, that she'd not given him a name. She'd told Lang at one point that the American was not as tall as he; but that was all he knew. He could go into her bedroom, and see if the diaphragm were there, but he did not go, because he knew that finding it in its place would give him no satisfaction. They had stopped sleeping together the autumn before last. He'd had several small affairs, actresses and the like, which meant nothing to him, something Thea had never understood. Now she considered herself estranged and had, in December, taken a lover. He could go to the bedroom, the top drawer, beneath the stockings. Of course it wouldn't be there. Ever since she found out, somehow, that he was in the habit of checking, she had taken to carrying the thing with her, everywhere. Above the fireplace were two small Otto Dix portraits of Thea, one full face, one three-quarters, which he preferred. To their right was a pre-Columbian figurine, bird-shaped, which had been given him by Professor Umlauff of the Ethnography Museum, whom he'd gotten to know while researching *Spiders*. He would have to go to Dahlem, soon, and retrieve the rest of the collection. Lang knew, clearly now, that he would not be living there again.

Closing his eyes, he saw railroad tracks, steel all agleam, converging in middle distance, toward a horizon never quite distinct. The wooden crossties came toward him, slowly at first, then with an increasing authority. He was quite low, just above the track bed, and the rails curved outward as they parted on either side. It was night. The track ahead was illuminated by what must have been the train's headlight, but as it picked up speed, the headlight never quite achieved the horizon, the point at which the rails had to meet. When he opened his eyes he realized he must have been asleep, though that hardly seemed the right word for it. He was having trouble lighting a cigarette when the telephone rang.

The telephone was in the next room.

He picked it up. It was the deskman, saying that a letter had been delivered by hand, and would Herr Lang prefer it to be brought up, or left at the desk, where he could collect it at his convenience?

"Bring it up," Lang said.

He went to his bedroom, and chose a smoking jacket of dark red silk with moiré lapels. Then he went to the door of his apartment and opened it. The shoes were shined. It had been done, silently, while he'd dozed by the hearth. Then the deskman came up, handed Lang an envelope. He seemed to linger fractionally before going off, as if expecting a tip, which was silly, because Lang, like all the tenants, took care of the staff quite generously, each Christmas. Lang went back to his chair where the cigarette, never properly lit, had gone out in its tray.

It was a handwritten note from Hugenberg, requesting the honor of Herr and Frau Lang at dinner the following evening, RSVP. A slightly yellowed newspaper clipping, folded in three, fluttered to the floor. It was from *Deutsche Allgemeine Zeitung*, one of Hugenberg's papers, and it was Hugenberg's personal editorial column. Lang inserted his monocle, pulled nearer the lamp by the side of the chair.

> During the election of 1930 I said: "Make the right wing strong! Thousands of people understood this as a demand that they vote for the Nazis, because "they are today's right wing." A short word about this: Today we, the German Nationalists, are still the right wing. No one exceeds us in the spirit of national reawakening. The struggle against Marxism and its supporters was led by my party of vision. Our basic economic and other programs are open for anyone to see. We need a national lifting of spirit and determination in Germany. But we also need sobriety and clarity in this time of confusion, hesitation, and extreme danger. Whoever wants to lead us, must make us strong. When I say, therefore, make the right wing strong, I mean make the German Nationalist Party strong.

At the bottom, in pen, in the white space provided by the top of a fashion advertisement, was the inscription, "One of my favorite columns, for one of my most *treasured* directors." The word "treasured" was underlined three times.

Lang picked up the phone. Reaching the desk, he asked if someone were waiting for a reply. "No, Herr Lang," said the deskman. "Is there some mistake?"

"Not at all," Lang told him. Without recradling the handpiece he flicked the hook, obtained a tone, and dialed from memory the home number of Dr. Humm, his dentist.

"Trouble?" Dr. Humm asked.

Lang explained the problem. Dr. Humm said he would fit Lang in the next afternoon, if Lang would attest that it was truly an emergency.

"I so attest," Lang told him and hung up. With a wrought-iron poker Lang toyed with the fire, which was low and sputtering. When he was satisfied, he placed a fresh log on top. Keeping his eye on the meticulous Dix portraits, he retreated backward to the chair. If he went out to eat, and did not drink coffee, sleep would be within reach by the time he returned. The fireside nap, just before the telephone rang, was unfortunate, but not of sufficient duration to spoil the night's rest. The dinner invitation could only be bad news. Lang was not sure of the reason a column had been enclosed, or of the decision behind the choice of this one in particular; but he did not have to be told what it meant when the man who owns the company which will distribute your film says you are *treasured*, in treble italics. It must have been Hugenberg in the projection booth, although Lang was under the impression Hugenberg had already seen it. The new log

2 5

was afire, and there was a crack as the one below it split in two. The light in the room trembled somewhat, as flames lapped the edges of the new log. There was light from the overhead, and from the reading lamp. The hearth shadows, then, were just at the threshold of what he could perceive. Abruptly he recalled something Brecht had said, at one of their conferences on *Threepenny*: "We must not say we were defeated because we were good, when in fact we were defeated because we were weak."

Lang could not recall the exact phrasing, which he was sure was more elegant, because Brecht honed his aphorisms, and gave them good, practiced readings. Lang wondered why he was remembering the line now, and just what it had to do with Hugenberg, with the tooth, with Thea. The railroad tracks, during his nap, had been coming toward him. More usually, they flowed away, stately, ultimate, wistful, as if seen from the hindmost car, looking back.

He stood up.

His shoes, which he'd retrieved when he'd gone to get the invitation, smelled of their fresh polish. Applying his nose to their bottoms, he thought he could detect the high tropical stench of aniline cement that they'd picked up from the new UFA carpet. It was a wonder he could smell anything, smoking as many cigarettes as he did.

Then there was the sound of a key ring being jangled, just outside the door. Lang heard the thin pulse of tumblers, and the heavier sound of the lock being turned.

Thea was in the doorway, all silhouette, a long trapezoid of spilled hallway light at her feet. She was wearing her black silk, with the pearls she'd inherited from her mother. Her father had bought them for her mother to mark their engagement, and now her mother was dead, and Thea wore them when she wished. Lang found himself glad that he was already standing, for he would have stood to greet her and might not have done it well.

"Fritz."

He put down the shoes. "Thea."

She walked toward him, kissed him high on the cheek, on her way to hang the heavy coat, already on her arm.

"Would you like some tea?" Lang said. "I could make some."

He heard her voice, husky and muffled, from within the closet: "No thank you."

She came back into the room, one hand on her hip. "I think," she told her husband, "I shall retire early." He could not get over the way her pale blue eyes worked against the white skin, the hair, now blue-black. "I have some reading I would like to do."

Lang tried to keep his face still, thought he was succeeding, but something must have showed, because Thea went to the vase, removing the rose.

"You were thinking I would be out all night," she told him.

"Yes."

He was sitting down now. She could come up behind the chair, place her hands on his shoulders. It would not have to promise anything.

"My hapless prosecutor," she said finally. He looked up to see her standing before the chair, the rose in her teeth. Then she set the rose on the table. "I was with Rudolf." She picked up the rose, made a dismissive gesture with her right hand.

"We're invited to dinner tomorrow night," Lang found himself saying. Thea looked at him. "At Hugenberg's," he went on.

"I thought you hated Hugenberg."

Lang looked away from her, toward the fireplace. It was burning well now. He did not look up to that part of the wall where he knew her portraits to be.

"Perhaps, if it's early enough. Probably not. I've a late date, which I don't want to break."

Lang knew, without having to ask, that she was to see her American. He was about to tell her of the Brechts, the scene at the train station, but did not want to hear the remarks she would make concerning it. He knew at once what Brecht had meant when he had hugged him and said, "We've lost." He did not know how to tell that to Thea. Thea was patriotic, had even embroidered, in fine thread, into the lining of her heavy coat, small colored shapes representing Germany's lost provinces.

"—reading," Thea was saying. And, when he looked up: "Good night."

He lit a cigarette, listened to her walk toward her bedroom, open the door, close it again.

"Good night," he responded a bit too loudly.

Lang went to his own bedroom, sat before the writing desk. He opened the ledger-sized diary, bound in black calf, found the next white page.

In 1920 Lang's first wife, a Russian Jew from Vilna, came upon Lang in the arms of Thea von Harbou, with whom Lang was collaborating on the screenplay for *Fighting Hearts*. The first Frau Lang went home and opened her wrists with her husband's straight razor. Lang was, at first, accused of murder. For the first time, he learned how tenuous reasons for suspicion can be; and because of this began his habit of noting down every event of his day, every telephone call, every visit, the menu of his meals.

Now he turned on the desk lamp, and proceeded to transcribe his activities for the last day of February, 1933, using the gold-nib fountain pen reserved, on an exclusive basis, for this task. The tooth seemed to hurt less now, and Lang was afraid that it would be all better by the time he saw Dr. Humm. He knew he would not sleep. Best, he thought, to go to Aschinger's, where everyone went "afterward" for breakfast, waiting on line, even at four A.M., unless they knew someone on the door. Hugenberg was a swine and Lang would call him, first thing in the morning, to decline the invitation. Lang wondered whether Hugenberg would insist, and whether he could get through the evening without Thea, and without having to answer too many questions from people who did not know him, about why she was not in attendence.

Lang went to the bathroom, removed his robe. Consulting the mirror, he recalled what he had told himself, in the Lancia, earlier in the evening, about needing a shave. He took off his shirt. There were two smallish, puckered scars high on the shoulder, where the bullets had gone in. They were still there. They always were. He had put on weight, and now the pudginess was showing in his face.

He ran the hot water, rotated the brush in its stream. The lighting in the bathroom was provided by a single overhead lamp. Lathering up, he moved close to the mirror, watched it fog where he breathed upon it. He wondered whether Thea had noticed the copy of *Die Dame* on the foyer table. He supposed he could knock on her door, but it was really too late now. With his left hand, he pulled taut the skin of his cheek, and with the right took up his pearl-handled razor. Soon his cheek was clean, and pink. He would have to lose some weight. "I would like," he told himself in the mirror, "to be able to shoot an illuminated forest in the middle of the night. Nobody has ever achieved that effect!"

T W O

DR. HUMM WORE A PARABOLIC REFLECTOR strapped to his forehead. In its center was a small bulb. Two thin wires draped downward from the headband. Lang traced them to a battery pack on Humm's belt. The thing was nowhere near as bright as the overhead lamp. Outside the office, on his way in, Lang had passed a street duo, one man at the harmonium, the other playing a bent saw with violin bow. He could just hear them now. Lang would have to find some way of informing Humm about the hairs which shot out from his nostrils. Their effect on patients in whom Humm wished to instill confidence. Lang's lip felt fat, and numb, from the procaine. Humm was holding a drill, connected by a series of lever arms, springs, pulleys, to an electric motor. There were two wads of rolled cotton in Lang's mouth, which he could no longer taste. Then Humm did something with the other hand, and the high, hideous motor began to whine.

"Open wide," Dr. Humm said. Lang tried to hear the street musicians over the motor, but could not. He looked up at Humm's reflector, his nose gone bulbous, forehead all distorted. The sound of the drill was inside his mouth now and he could feel Humm going at the molar, right-side bottom. Lang felt fragments of tooth dust, spun outward by the drill, hit the side of his tongue. There was a taste, or a smell really, at the back of his throat, of something burnt.

"Rinse out," Humm was saying, as he removed the cotton wadding.

"That it?" Lang asked in facetious expectancy.

"Oh no," said Humm, failing to catch, it seemed, Lang's little joke. He repacked Lang's mouth with fresh wadding. Lang made out a few bars of "Pirate Jenny," arranged for saw and harmonium, before the motor started up again.

"Relax," said Humm. Lang wondered who the man in the projection booth had been if not Hugenberg who, he was sure now, had already seen it. Kallman, UFA's president, with whom Lang had gone to New York ten years ago, was off skiing in Switzerland. Correll had seen it several times.

"You're not relaxing," Humm was saying. Lang felt the vibration as Humm went at the tooth; and then pain, sharp, sudden, unexpected. It seemed to illuminate, like chain lightning, everything inside him.

"Hurt?" Humm asked.

Lang nodded.

"Hurt a lot?"

"Yes," Lang managed to say.

The doctor smiled. "The nerve is not dead yet. Good news for you, my friend." He flicked the motor on once more.

"No," said Lang. He watched his face reflected, fun house style, in the parabolic headpiece. There was something quite funny about the way his own lips had moved, in the mirror, when he'd formed the word "no." Humm extracted the cotton.

After rinsing out, Lang said, "I am a coward about physical pain."

"The nerve is alive," Humm replied.

Lang said nothing.

"Merely," Humm went on, gesturing casually, the forgotten drill still in hand, as if unaware just how menacing his emphasis must seem, "that you will feel it. With more anesthetic you will feel it less. But feel it you will."

Lang searched out, with forefinger, fragments of tooth, seemingly quite large, which he could still feel in the pouch between cheek and gum. The water in the porcelain bowl, into which he spit, jetted counterclockwise, as if designed for use below the equator.

"You would not want me," Humm was saying, "to lie to you." He had finally let go the drill, which bobbed about on its pantograph arm.

Lang held his finger before him. He could not grasp how the fragments, so large against his gum, could be so minuscule, no more than sand grains, out here in the light. You could, Lang supposed, consider the twin sprays of hair sent out by Humm's nostrils as part of his mustache, but you'd have to be nearsighted, or dishonest with yourself, to see it that way. Hearing the saw and harmonium once more, playing a folk air whose name he knew but which was just beyond his grasp, Lang looked toward the window. He could see nothing through fully closed wooden slats of Venetian blinds. Lang had shot two versions of *Testament*, one in German, one in French, with a somewhat differing cast. Nebenzal had hired an editor to conform the French version to Lang's cut of the German, and Lang supposed he could do some playing around there. Usually he would have flung himself into something else by now. But he was, as they say, between films, and sitting in Humm's diabolical chair, he recalled at once something he'd known for years, that he was never really happy, unless working. The duo was playing from *Threepenny* again.

"—laughing gas," Humm was saying. Lang had no idea how long Humm had been talking.

"It makes me giddy," Lang told him, feigning attentiveness. "Light-headed, in an unpleasant way."

"Just as I said," Humm interrupted, and Lang wondered how evident it was that his thoughts had been elsewhere for some length of time. "Would you prefer ether?" Humm was asking.

"Will it put me out?"

"Quite."

"By all means," Lang said finally. The back of his neck was aching. He reached back to adjust the headrest, which had been set for a patient previous, someone shorter. Humm bent down, sliding the tambour doors on the lower cabinet. Lang watched him remove a glass liter bottle, with ground-glass stopper, and an oval mask of wire mesh.

"Relax," Humm said once more. "I'm going to place this lightweight mask over your nose and mouth." He went on as if quoting. "Then I will tell you that a feather has landed on the tip of your nose, and you want to blow it off. You will close your eyes, and relax, and try to dislodge the feather, which has settled annoyingly on the very tip of your nose." His recitation became slightly singsong, as if lecturing a kindergarten.

When Humm seemed to be finished, Lang said, "I understand."

"Good," said Humm, placing the mask over Lang's nose and mouth. Lang watched him cover the mask with a piece of toweling.

"Close your eyes."

Lang closed them.

"Just relax."

Lang found a comfortable place for his fingers on the side of the leather padded arms of Humm's chair.

"Now blow that feather!"

It was, Lang realized, a clever way to get him to inhale. He almost said something, but he did not want to embarrass Humm by letting him know just how transparent his shoddy little ruse was, to an adult. Besides, it was too late now. The mask would muffle anything he had to say.

The ether was sweet, overwhelmingly so, like gardenias, or the aniline cement in the UFA screening room; but after a while Lang found it less difficult to take the ether all the way down, hold it there. He saw twin wheels of wire mesh—much the same material of which the mask was made—spinning against each other, the left clockwise, the right counterclock, and the small silhouette of a man at their juncture, growing smaller.

He had been filming Thea's scenarios for ten years, and had forgotten what writing might be like, without her. Sometimes when they had worked together they had not been on the best of terms; but things were different now, and he could not visualize the two of them at their desk.

The wheels were spinning more slowly. Lang could see ripples, and moirés, in the pointed oval where the disks intersected. Then he discerned once more the silhouette of a man walking, it seemed, down a railroad track, becoming smaller but not, somehow, more distant. He could see the tracks now. The crossties sank below him, one by one. Sprocket holes appeared, at the ties' outer edges. For a while he was unsure whether he were looking at a railroad track or a strip of film. The rectangles sank, one by one. The silhouetted man became still more tiny. Then the spinning disks reasserted themselves, obliterating all between them. There was a horrible grinding sound as the disks grated against one another.

Lang opened his eyes. Humm had evidently adjusted the blinds: slats of light fell diagonal and precise across the wall, floor, chair. He watched Humm, by the window, preparing something with mortar and pestle. Lang wanted to reach up and see if the wire mesh was still covering his mouth, but he found his hand and arm too heavy to lift. Lang closed his eyes. He recalled the man who had been bowing the bent saw, and who had worn a cloth cap, a shawl-collared sweater. It was not an outfit warm enough for the weather outside—bright enough, but just above freezing. Then Lang was falling. It was as if he had been reclining in a barber chair in the clouds whose operator had decided to lower it all the way back down.

He was awake for some time before opening his eyes. It was something he would do as a child, on Sunday mornings. See how long he could lie in bed, awake, without letting them know he could hear every word.

The oblique slats of light were still falling across his legs and chest. Lang moved his head, and his eyes were no longer in shadow. Humm was still at work with the pestle. Lang could not decide whether the grinding sound, in his reverie, had been produced by the drill or the mortar.

"I am combining silver with mercury in an amal-gam," Humm was reciting. "How do you feel?"

Lang tried to talk, but found his tongue blocked by cotton wadding. He grunted affirmatively.

"You will experience," Humm went on, "some dis-orientation, with which you should not be alarmed. Should it persist for any period of time, feel free to contact this office." Lang watched the crisp Venetian shadow play up and down Humm's forearm as he prepared the amalgam. "Cocaine is an anæsthetic, but it also has tonic properties, and I can give you some to take with you, to counteract any drowsiness you might perceive."

Lang nodded.

"Now we seal the cavity with this"—he held up a small bottle of light-brown liquid—"which may be thought of as shellac. Then the amalgam, which I shall sculpt in a likeness of those surfaces of the tooth which had to be removed, when I went in, to search out all rot." Lang listened intently for the saw, the harmonium, heard noth-ing, save loud conversation, among several people, the words of which did not seem to carry through Humm's storm window.

"You seem inattentive, Herr Lang. It is better that you understand the reason for our work today." Humm dipped a fine paintbrush in the small bottle, commenced to coat the cavity. Lang stared once more into the reflec-tor. He supposed he should be grateful to Humm for saving the tooth. There was a resinous taste in his mouth, spreading right to left. It was not unpleasant. Occasionally, when he breathed, the burnt-bone smell would come back, high at the top of his throat.

"Now for the art," said Humm, scooping amalgam

with a miniature trowel. Lang closed his eyes, giving himself over to Humm's care.

Set into the waiting room wall was a gas hearth, protected by vertical cast-iron grating. It splayed distinct, regular shadows across the room's solid carpet. Lang played a game of childhood, trying hard not to step on the "lines." He had made it to the coatrack when he heard Humm's voice.

"Don't chew on the right side for several hours," the doctor announced. The reflector was still strapped to his head. At some point he'd turned off the bulb, conserving battery life. There were two men on the waiting room couch who had not removed their hats. The one on the right had a scar which ran from the corner of his eye to the edge of his mouth. The other moved his large hands in outsize gestures, and had the chronically blank aspect of a deaf-mute.

"For the pain," said Humm, tossing Lang a small cardboard box. Lang caught it easily, left-handed, but had to step on a line in order to do so.

"Thanks," he said automatically. He waited briefly, while putting on his leather coat, for either man to enter Humm's office. They made no move to stand, or to remove their hats, as Lang closed the waiting room door.

Outside he found himself immediately at the edge of a fair-sized crowd. He could hear an ambulance or police siren approaching. The crowd seemed to be assembled circularly, as if around something.

"What happened?" Lang asked a man in a Tyrolean hat, one foot off the curb.

"Five minutes ago," the man said, moving on. An ambulance had pulled up. Onlookers made way. Lang stopped an elderly woman who seemed to be backing away from the center of the thing.

"What is the story?"

"It was terrible," she said. "They beat him up."

"You didn't see it," said another woman, apparently her companion.

"But I heard his partner," the first woman said.

Lang was able to see over several heads, and in the gaps between shoulders, to where the ambulance attendants were rolling out a canvas litter. The man they were loading onto it was the man who had been playing the harmonium. His face was all blood and bandages; his left arm stuck out at an unnatural angle. Lang told himself that if he left now he might still catch Thea before she went off with her American. The saw player, one hand to the top of his head, was saying "Get away" to the attendants. They had the litter in the ambulance now. The saw player continued to wave them off, quite furiously, with his free hand.

"Call the police?" he was shouting, incredulous. Lang supposed him in some sort of shock. "Call the police?"

"Clear the street. Everything is over," one of the attendants was saying. He wore a pointed kepi, and Lang could not tell if he were some sort of official. Lang worked his way to the front. Blood was dripping, in thick painterly rivulets, from the top of the saw player's head, to which he was holding a handkerchief, or perhaps a piece of gauze.

"There's nothing to see," the man in the kepi was saying. Looking over his shoulder, Lang saw the crowd no smaller now than when he had arrived.

"Swine," the saw player said to no one in particular. Then the ambulance began to pull out, and the saw player scrambled for the rear door, to ride with his companion. A man in a sailor's coat sat on the curb, tying and untying his shoelaces repeatedly. His right eye was purple, swollen. Lang sat down next to him.

"What happened?" Lang asked softly. The ambulance, gathering speed now, had put on its siren.

"They were playing from *Threepenny*," the man said, "when the brownshirts passed."

"Are you all right?" Lang heard himself ask.

The man said nothing.

"I was in the dentist's," Lang said finally, rising. There was still a small crowd, two deep around a semicircle of vacant curb and cobblestone, where something had happened.

"Nothing to see," the official repeated. Then Lang found himself picturing the man with the scar, from Humm's waiting room, behind the wheel of a Mercedes, such as the one which had followed him, through several consecutive turns, the night previous. But he had not seen the Mercedes's driver, and had no reason to suppose he had seen the scar-faced man before, anywhere.

"Are you sure," Lang bent to ask the man in the navy wool sailor coat, "there's nothing I can do?"

The man, busy with his shoelace, did not hear, or at any rate made no response. Finally Lang went off, finding himself walking down Kochstrasse in the direction of his car. Lang's mother Paula, though Jewish, had been raised as a Roman Catholic, and had reared her son with a convert's zeal. The most important of Lang's childhood memories, which he replayed for himself with some regularity, was of the Christkindlmarkt. On a low wooden platform only a step or two higher than the cobbled pavement, there were simple wooden stalls filled with inexpensive Christmas toys. As the passageways between the stalls were roofed over as well, it was possible, even during a snowstorm, to walk about the stalls amid many colorful candles and oil lamps. There were wonderful things to buy: jolly Christmas tree decorations, glass balls and stars and garlands of silvered tinsel and red-cheeked apples and golden oranges and dates; fantastic toys, rocking horses and puppets and Punch and Judy and tin soldiers; toy theaters with characters and scenes for many different plays. Then there was the Wurstlprater with a ferris wheel, shooting ranges, sideshows, and merry-go-rounds. Now, seated before the controls of his Lancia, warming the engine against the chill, he ran the images, as one might fondle in reassurance the threadbare favored blanket. A police car passed, on its way, apparently, to the disturbance. A sweep of light, from the scarlet rotating reflector atop, hit Lang full in the eyes, and he closed them tightly as he listened to the siren recede, ever fainter, and lower in pitch than it had been on approach. The engine was warm now. Scanning the gauges, Lang saw the gas at the one-quarter mark, and told himself to remember to stop at the Shell station before pulling in for the night. It occurred to him that he had left his monocle in Dr. Humm's office. He patted his jacket and fished the four small pockets in his vest, confirming the loss. He recalled quite precisely now taking the glass out, and placing it on the side table, before settling into Humm's pneumatic recliner. He did not want to go back. There was another, at home; and a third, in his rolltop at the Nero Films office. Lang wondered what Thea's American did for a living. Engaging the clutch, he pulled his roadster forward, easing it skillfully into traffic.

He had parked the car in one of the spaces reserved for residents when he recalled he'd not stopped at the Shell station. Unhappy to find himself under spells of forgetfulness, he would have taken it for a bad sign, were there not the ether, and its aftereffects, to which to ascribe them. Slamming the door of the Lancia he recalled the box of cocaine in his left coat pocket. Perhaps it would wake him up.

"Josef, would you mind," Lang inquired of his doorman, handing him the car keys, "running the car down to the station? I'm afraid I've left her low on gas."

"Anything Herr Lang desires," said the doorman. Lang essayed a smile of thanks, went through the door.

"Just this, I'm afraid," the deskman told him, handling over a solitary letter, and adding a moment later, "Frau Lang is out." Lang tried to read the voice, to see if he were being humiliated, but the deskman's inflection had been flat, and there was no way Lang could accuse him. He turned for the stairs.

Inside, he slid his thumb along the envelope's wide flap. It was a note from Max Ophuls, whom Lang had met socially a few times, and whose film *Liebelei*, a tale of doomed lovers, he'd seen on New Year's Day. It was quite marvelous. In the letter, Ophuls wrote that he "felt it best to remove his family to France," giving a Paris address where he could be contacted. Ophuls was perhaps ten years younger than he, and Lang recalled having been told that he had changed his name, from Oppenheimer, ostensibly so as not to embarrass his family, when embarking upon a career in show business. He would have to write Ophuls, at the new address, to tell him how much he liked the film.

42

Lang was seated in his favorite chair, crafting lines of cocaine with his straight razor upon the blue-glass table, the way he'd seen it done in the social clubs, when the phone went off. Rising to pick it up he heard, between rings, the jangle of keys just outside the door. He cradled the receiver against his shoulder, lighting a Boyard which tasted better now that the anæsthetic was wearing off. His wife was in the doorway.

"Just one moment," he said into the phone, realizing he'd no idea who was calling. "Hello," he said, in another voice, one hand cupped over the mouthpiece.

"Good evening," said Thea. She was wearing a black fur coat, heels inappropriately high for walking in this kind of weather, with the streets prone to ice.

"Sorry," he said into the phone, squinting against the smoke which drifted harshly up from the fat cigarette.

"I am sending a car into the city to fetch guests. Can you be ready at eight?"

"Eight," Lang repeated.

"Good then," said the voice, and rang off. It had been Hugenberg. Lang had forgotten to cancel. He stared at the phone, dead in his hand.

"A present?" Thea was asking. She was seated in the red leather chair, his favorite, next to the tabletop.

"Medicinal purposes only," he told her. He replaced the phone. Lang could tell by her mouth, and the way she sat, that Thea was in good spirits.

"Let us," she said, extracting from her purse the ebony cigarette holder, removing its hollow brass ferrule.

"Oh yes," Lang said. He watched her stand, remove the coat, fling it toward the couch. She hovered low, above the blued mirror glass. She inhaled two lines, handed

43

the ferrule to him. He could feel her breath on the top of his head as he bent over the table.

"You've been to Humm," she said, tapping the small cardboard box.

"Yes." He did not want to lift his head just yet.

"What did he do to you?" she asked, hand suddenly on his shoulder.

"Right rear," he told her, opening his mouth to show off the newest filling.

"He didn't hurt you, did he?"

"Not badly. He gave me ether."

She inhaled another line. "Let's not talk about Humm."

Lang almost said "You brought it up," quite automatically, but somehow held back. He was a bit surprised, actually, when the words didn't come. Thea handed him the tube. The edge of her hair, blue-black, grown out now to jawline length, brushed against the bone on the outside of his wrist. He told himself to remember that the drug was pharmaceutical, likely to be quite strong.

Thea reclined, once more, in the leather chair.

Lang bent low over the tabletop.

He worked to keep from saying something, for fear it would be the wrong thing, and Thea would get up, walk to her own room, where she would prepare herself for the American. Lang had little use for music, but wished now for a string quartet, something atmospheric. When she handed the ferrule back to him, he would see if she continued to hold it momentarily after he'd got a grip on it. Then he would know.

"Who was that on the phone?"

"Hugenberg," Lang said finally. The backs of his thighs were beginning to tremble from bending low over the table. He went for the other chair, pulling it a bit closer, and angling it toward his wife. "He's sending his car," Lang went on distractedly, glad now to be making words, "at eight. I think he was afraid I would invoke auto trouble at the last minute." The sound of his own voice pleased him for the first time in days. It was strong, with a nice feel for the ironic. "I thought I saw Erich yesterday," he continued, "at the railway station, but it couldn't have been him, unless he lied about being sick."

"Perhaps he lied."

He watched points of light, at the edge of the molding along the wall, and in the convexities of the Dix portraits' figured metal frames. There was a woman named Lily he had been seeing something of. He could call her, make a date for later tonight. He would be able to write it up, in his diary, in a way which would make it clear he was not behaving badly. Lang struck a wooden match, gazed at it awhile, until he could feel the heat of its flame at his thumb.

"Pass me a light, please. What shall I wear to Hugenberg's?"

He tossed her a box of wax matches someone had brought from Paris. "The gray dress," he said flatly, trying to keep from his voice the relief that she would accompany him.

"Not the gray."

"The black and white."

"Better," Thea said. He did not want to ask why she'd changed her mind about the evening.

"Have I told you," he found himself asking, and was immediately sorry, even as he said it, that he'd let the words out, "how much I love you?"

Thea said, "Yes." She was bent over the table again. Her hair covered the side of her face, and he could not see her lips as they formed the reply. He could only hope he'd not ruined all.

"The man had Erich's walk, at any rate. In the station," he heard himself going on.

"I must change," said Thea, rising from the chair. Abruptly she was gone, into her bedroom. He had not caught sight of her face full on since he'd said the thing he shouldn't have said. He tried to hear it again, wondering if the tone were casual enough for him to have gotten away with it. He promised himself a new set of oils, this summer. (He'd not touched the old wooden paintbox, somewhere in Dahlem, in a year or two. The brushes were probably all stiff.) Then he was before the sink, looking at a cup, saucer, two flat dishes. He took the apron from the rack, pulled it over his head, tied the strings behind himself. He did not want to wet his shirt, the favorite voile, still fresh enough to wear tonight.

The wall in front of the sink was white. Lang stared into it, hands blindly moving over the china. Hearing a noise he looked off to his right, saw only the doorway and the living room lamp beyond. Then he looked back to the white wall, savoring the lamp's afterimage, floating in front of him the way the shade of Mabuse hovered above possessed Professor Baum. Lang found himself recalling with pleasure the sequence in *Testament* in which we come upon several cars, stopped for a red light. The light turns green. We watch the left and right lanes of traffic flow through the intersection. The middle lane seems stalled. The front car has not noticed that the light has changed. Other cars swerve around it, honking mercilessly. Then we see Doctor Kamm slumped over the wheel, and know that Mabuse has once more done his hideous work. Or has had it performed by surrogates, on his evil behalf. Lang racked the dishes.

Still wearing the apron, Lang retrieved the razor from the living room. In his bedroom mirror, Lang saw a faint blue stubble along the jawline, which he decided would be fine, especially on someone artistic. He picked a dark foulard tie, deftly threading a four-in-hand. Thea would be out of her dress by now, seated in full slip before the vanity, with its outsized round mirror. He could image her moving nearer the glass to check her mascara, silk underpants sliding with unexpected smoothness against silk slip. The death of Doctor Kamm had been written by Thea, given to him the morning of the shoot, almost as a gift. She would be holding the mascara brush lightly now, between thumb and forefinger. The elbow would be back, for balance, thrusting up the collarbone, which would strain against the slip's thin strap. The small concavity between collarbone and neck which that strap would bridge, just taut enough so as not to touch the skin beneath. The shadow which the strap would cast, on that untouched piece of skin.

Lang untied the apron, removed it, flung it against the wall with a good deal of force. At the door to Thea's bedroom he knocked twice and, without waiting for reply, entered. She was nowhere to be seen.

"Fritz?" Her voice came muffled from within the deep closet. She repeated his name, emerged, holding the black-and-white dress in front of her. She did not appear to be wearing anything behind it but fullish deep-red tap pants.

Lang sat on her bed, placing his large face between his hands.

"Let us not have to do this again," said Thea softly. He looked up to see her grab a black slip, not at all the peach-colored one he had visualized, back in his room. She raised it above her head, disappeared for a moment, then wriggled, tugged, smoothing the garment about herself.

He replaced his head between his hands. "I can't take it," he said huskily.

"Yes you can," his wife told him. She sat beside him. Looking up once more he could see himself, and Thea, two room lengths away, framed by the circular vanity glass. They seemed small, oddly formal. "Yes you can," she repeated, the back of her hand rubbing up and down the nape of his neck.

"I don't want you to see him," Lang said finally.

"We've been through this."

"You're seeing him tonight."

"I'm dining with you tonight. Then I'll be going out. Later. You do it all the time."

He looked at her. "I'm sorry." He could see in the far mirror that his tie was askew, and adjusted it. "Do you know," he went on after a bit, "how difficult this is for me?"

"No one tells me who I can sleep with anymore," she said unemphatically, as if by rote. Then, at once, they were reaching for cigarettes. Thea fitted one of hers into the long, polished ebony holder, reassembled now. Lang tamped a Boyard against a thumbnail. He held a match for his wife, for himself. It was seven. Perhaps he could get her to feel some tenderness for him, in the hour before they left. (Someday he wanted to sleep with her, just prior to her departure for the American. He thought of the diaphragm, which she'd insert, and carry with her, as his message to the other man.) Then at once his mood lifted, and he felt like nothing more than to tell his wife a story.

"The open sky country," he said. "Texas. We are watching the fairest woman in all the land. She is wandering in the moonlight beyond the town, looking for her lover, when Destiny arrives, and takes off his hat."

Thea went to the dresser, extracted a pair of stockings, which she unraveled, and drew on, left leg first.

"She spins a thousand and one tales, knowing he will not take her lover, as long as she can keep his attention." He could see the outline of the deep-red pants, beneath the slip, as she bent to affix her garters. Perhaps the American had given them to her. He really didn't know. "Her first tale is of the archfiend, the hapless prosecutor. The professor who falls under the archfiend's spell. The professor's daughter, of course."

"Am I to be the most beautiful woman under the big sky," Thea asked as she sat on the low bench before the vanity, "or the professor's daughter?"

"One actress for the both, of course," Lang said. He wondered how large the dinner at Hugenberg's would be. It might be more tolerable with hundreds of guests. He could be social, working oiled and gracious from one clot to the next.

Thea said, "Do you get to be Destiny, as well as the archfiend?"

"Yes." He put his head on her pillow, stretching his legs, letting slippers fall to the rug. Thea was bringing in the blue-glass table. It was braced against her thighs, and she took small, comic steps, moving from the knee down.

49

Light from the overhead bounced off the tabletop, casting a stuttering blue streak on the ceiling.

She set the table down before them, like a breakfast tray. The white nebulae had not spilled. He watched the shadow of her head carve a corner from the pale blue rectangle on the ceiling. (He'd always been in favor of single-source lighting for indoor scenes.) It was Lang's turn, and he inhaled deeply. Thea's thigh was perhaps two millimeters from his, alongside, on the bed. He knew that if he were to shift weight slightly, so that they touched, she would take her time before finding that gesture which would make it necessary for her to pull away.

They lit a second round of cigarettes.

"I don't see you," Thea said, looking straight ahead, presenting him her left profile, "as the archfiend."

"No?" He raised his eyebrows, screwing up his nose, and forming his tongue in a gargoyle-style trefoil. It was a face he learned, when he was ten, that not everyone could make.

"No." Thea smiled broadly, pushing the tip of her nose upward with a forefinger.

Then they were looking at each other, and they were not making faces, other than their own.

Thea told him, "You will always be my hapless prosecutor."

She set down the cigarette holder. It had been a prop, used by Countess Told, in the original *Mabuse*. Lang tried to recall the name of the actress who had played the Countess. Gertrude Welcker.

Lang looked at her.

He buried his lips at the base of his wife's neck, in the soft triangle just above the collarbone. He could feel her blue-black hair at the side of his cheek. When Thea exhaled he felt it as a warm breeze across his brow. Then he knew, by the rhythm of that breeze, she was about to cry. Lang pulled away, to see his wife's pale blue eyes fill, become watery. A first tear broke loose, leaving a damp trail from the eye's outside corner. Halfway down her cheek it stopped, spent. Thea wiped her eyes with the back of her hand. She was not sobbing.

"Don't cry," Lang found himself saying miserably. A week earlier, before she was leaving, Lang had reduced her to tears, so that the other man would know by her reddened face that she was still married, had a husband who could still get to her. But he did not want to make her cry now. He turned his head to see her breathing quick and shallow once more, as if she might let go. He felt a fold of flesh, pinched by the collar of his shirt, ran a finger between neckband and neck to free it. It was important what the American thought of him. Looking in the far circular mirror Lang undid his collar. He had to take off some weight.

"I can't take this," Thea was saying, in a low, uninflected voice. Her hands, clasped in front of her, rested on the center of the table. Thea's forearms shone cool and still beneath the virtual surface of the blued mirror.

Lang and Thea both lit new cigarettes.

He stood up, adjusting the way his shirt bloused over the sides of his waistband. Lang said, "We had better get dressed."

Thea said nothing.

Without shutting her door, Lang walked to his own room. From the right-hand side of his dresser he selected a pair of thin silk hose. They were sheer glossy black with slim vertical ribbing. He and Thea had talked, at one time, of taking a vacation, in Vienna, and Italy perhaps, where Lang had fought in the war. "After the film," Thea had said; but there had been no plans made beyond that, and they had neither of them mentioned it since *Testament*'s completion. It seemed to Lang now quite unlikely they'd go away together. He tried on a pair of patent evening slippers, but judged them wrong for the trousers. Instead he took out the shoes he'd worn the day before, which had picked up the stench of aniline cement from the new UFA carpet. He brought one close, but could smell nothing objectionable now. He ran a fingertip across his cheek, pleased with his decision not to shave. He went to the closet, reached high, for his cummerbund. His hand found, instead, an old scrapbook.

He sat on the bed, opened at random. There was an article he'd written describing his first impression, from aboard the S.S. *Deutschland*, of New York:

> . . . the crossroads of multiple and confused human forces, irresistibly driven to exploit each other and thus live in perpetual anxiety. I saw a street lit as if in full daylight by neon lights, and topping them oversized luminous advertisements moving, turning, flashing on and off, spiraling. . . . The buildings seemed to be a vertical veil, shimmering, almost weightless, a luxurious cloth hung from the dark sky to dazzle, distract, and hypnotize. At night the city did not give the impression of being alive; it lived as illusions lived. I knew then that I had to make a film about all of these sensations.

There was a photograph, from the American trip, of him and Lubitsch in Los Angeles, Lang in the pool, Lubitsch clowning with Lang's monocle. Another photo, perhaps a year later, from the *Metropolis* period: himself behind a set of drums, Thea at the piano, actress Brigitte Helm holding a sax. He couldn't remember now why they had taken that one. Lang closed the large book. Then he found himself once more at the doorway of Thea's room.

She was at her vanity, applying eye shadow, in a pose similar to the one he had imaged earlier. He came up behind her, fixing the cloth-covered buttons on the back of Thea's black-and-white dress, the ones she could never quite reach herself.

Thea took a drag on the ebony holder, exhaled slowly. She met her husband's eyes briefly in the mirror before concentrating once more on her makeup.

"Are you all right," Lang asked, careful that it not come out too loudly.

"Yes." She was applying rouge now, with a beaver brush, rather like a shaving brush, Lang thought, but about one-third the size. He sat down beside her on the low bench, keeping his back erect.

"Can I get you anything?"

"No thank you," said Thea, not meeting his eyes. She took up her cigarette.

"Don't be this way," he said finally, his voice strong once more. There was a dull ache in his jaw, but nothing like the painful throb before he'd gone to Humm. It occurred to Lang that if they were beating people in the street for playing songs from *Threepenny*, Brecht was probably right to be leaving.

"Isn't this what you wanted," Thea was saying.

"What do you mean."

Thea was looking at him, in the mirror.

"This is not what I wanted," he said finally, in his best voice. Then the phone was ringing. Lang went to the extension on Thea's night table.

"Hugenberg's car is downstairs," he said after hanging up.

"See you later then," said Thea without turning around.

Often, after a bout of sadness, Thea would get like this; and Lang knew there was nothing he could do but wait. It was not something she could keep up for more than a few days at one stretch. Lang said evenly, "You're not coming, then?"

"I have to take the Lancia anyway, in case I have to leave before the evening is over. I shall meet you there."

For a moment Lang wanted to tell her not to do him any favors: he was not sure how much of a comfort she'd be, at his side, like this. Turning, he found himself gazing at the narrow strip of nape flesh, between the bottom of her hair, the top of the dress. Maintaining his gaze as if held, he found himself awash in a wave of poignance. The lights in the room—all over the world, perhaps—went soft, atmospheric. Then he was able to pull away, gaze instead at the vista of hallway, hearth, living room, alive with depth and color, framed by Thea's doorway.

"See you there," he said mechanically, walking toward that doorway, not daring to look anywhere but ahead. At the closet he put on his cutaway, and took out the black wool overcoat. Then he was descending the oversized, slightly curved staircase which led to the lobby. The mahogany banister shone, and was sleek to the touch. Lang thought he could detect the odor of tung oil lingering somewhere in the dank stairwell air.

Outside it was snowing gently, large flakes, which settled on the brim of his homburg. The uniformed driver was standing just outside the streetlamp's cone of light, holding open the rear door. Lang entered the cabriolet expecting, for no reason at all really, to find himself alone, when the other man said, "Fritz."

"Seymour." Seymour Nebenzal, a compact Jew about ten years Lang's junior, had produced Lang's last two films. "I see they roped you in as well," Lang went on. Nebenzal was attempting a thin mustache, which looked like an anchovy. He told himself to remember to ask Nebenzal to return his favorite Karl May book, which he'd been missing of late.

"I was about to decline, Fritz, when the car arrived." The uniformed driver was making his way around the front of the car. "I've always been intimidated by livery," Nebenzal continued. Lang removed his hat, knocking off snowflakes, before they could melt, staining the silk hatband. The driver started up the engine. Lang found himself returning once more to the memory of colored Christmas lights.

Nebenzal said, "Hugenberg tells me, 'I need an Easter film for the Palast. Get Lang to make me another *Mabuse*.' I tell him, 'You want dance, crime, gambling, passion, cocaine addiction, jazz, stock exchange manuevers, occultist charlatanism, prostitution, overeating, smuggling, hypnosis, counterfeiting, violence, murder, Expressionism?' He nodded, said, 'Yes, yes, yes!' " It was that part of the memory where he passed the stand where you could buy small toys, with the special coins your father had given you. "But I think," Nebenzal was going on, "he didn't really want another *Mabuse* after all. At least not one in which all the criminals talk like Nazis. 'Steal not one penny from the people,' says this new Mabuse: 'We must create a realm of pure crime.' Now what, Fritz, is Hugenberg going to think *that's* about?"

Lang realized that the car was not moving. He looked up.

"We are waiting for your wife," Nebenzal said finally, with rising inflection, almost a question.

"She'll be arriving separately," said Lang distractedly. Then Lang said, "Wait!" and was out the door.

Out of breath at the top of the stairs, Lang opened his door, which he'd forgotten to lock on the way out.

He went through the hallway, and the living room, to the door which led to his wife's bedroom. Lang entered it, and found it empty. The sound of running water came from the bathroom. He wondered how long she would take, and if he would have time for the final word with her alone, without leaving Nebenzal to wait in the car for an intolerable period. Then he was sitting on the bed, telephone in hand, asking the operator to connect him with Earl Pfeiffer, whose address he did not know.

"Pfeiffer," said Lang, when the connection was made.

"Yes?"

"Lang here. I want you to tell me right now, and to tell me with honesty, whom you were hiding in the projection booth yesterday." Lang was immediately pleased with his choice of words, with the strength of his voice.

Pfeiffer told him that there had been someone in the projection booth, that he would have told Lang on the spot, that—

"I'm just now walking out the door. Don't make me late."

Pfeiffer's voice on the telephone was thin, tinny, removed. It was as if he'd already spoken his words hours before. "It was Doctor Goebbels."

The water in the bathroom was still running. "Did he enjoy it?" Lang said finally, keeping his inflection flat.

"He seemed to, Herr Lang. For the most part he seemed to like it quite well."

"Go on."

"I'm not sure, Herr Lang, that it's right—"

Lang asked, "Did he say anything?"

"—when Mabuse dies."

"Yes?" Mabuse is last seen in his asylum cell, churning out on sheet after sheet of paper his plans for hurling mankind into an "abyss of terror," when he collapses, terminally spent.

Pfeiffer coughed twice. Lang could hear, in the background, a small child, demanding something insistently. "He said that was not the way it should happen. He said a mob should storm the asylum. That Mabuse must be destroyed by the will of the people."

"Thank you, Pfeiffer. I appreciate your help." Lang was aware, to some extent, that Pfeiffer was going on, but the phone was in front of him now, and he could not discern what the man was saying. Then the phone was back in its cradle. Lang was at Thea's dresser. He slid the drawer, and lifted stockings, to see if the diaphragm were in its place. Abruptly the distant running water changed its pitch and Lang closed the drawer, taking care that its front was flush with the veneer of the one

57

below it. He went over to the table with the cocaine upon it.

Lang went out the door, down the stairs, through the lobby, outside. Before he knew it he was back in the car. "My monocle," he explained to Nebenzal as he sat down, once more, in the rear of the cabriolet. Nebenzal tapped on the pane of glass which separated the two compartments. The driver engaged the clutch.

"I'd forgotten my monocle," Lang said. Nebenzal looked at him. Nebenzal's coat was damp and gave off the smell of wet wool. Lang considered opening a window, decided against it, recalling how cold it had been outside. He was glad now that he'd not waited for his wife to emerge from the bathroom although that was, he remembered now, the reason he had gone back upstairs. He hitched the knees of his trousers. They were on Kaiserdamm now, lamps on either side sweeping by with a regularity Lang found reassuring. It was possible the diaphragm was deeper in the drawer than he'd had time to search, but more likely she'd already transferred it to her purse. Now Lang was aware that the car had stopped; that there were red and white lights; that words had passed between the driver and a uniformed officer. Then they were turning off Kaiserdamm to a one-lane cross street, badly paved.

"Did you catch that?" Lang asked, risking that Nebenzal might realize he'd been somewhere else again.

Nebenzal said, "A small riot, around which we've been asked to detour." He offered a cigarette from an enamel and silver case, which Lang waved away. "The sight of a car like this one," Nebenzal went on, "is not good, for the rioters." Lang watched Nebenzal let smoke escape from his mouth, reinhale it through his nostrils, in the French manner. At Hugenberg's, if Thea went at any point to another room without taking her purse, he could examine it surreptitiously. Run his long fingers along the pliant kidskin surface to seek out, in a Braille of betrayal, that distinctive circular shape beneath. They had made another turn, onto a better-lit street, Kantstrasse perhaps, which seemed to parallel their intended route.

"Not at all good for them," Nebenzal was saying.

Lang recalled that he had been in a riot, in Vienna; but as he found himself speaking, in a lively conversational tone, it was not of Vienna at all. "On my first day of shooting *Halfbreed* for Joe May," Lang was saying, "my car was detained on the way to the studio, a warehouse in some northern industrial suburb." Lang looked at Nebenzal, whom he hadn't seen since the holidays, and was surprised how old his friend seemed. There was a distinct separation now between his chin and the line of his jaw. When he smiled the lines at the side of his mouth went all the way down. The mustache was not successful. "It was Spartacus week," Lang continued. "Nineteen-nineteen. My very first film, mind you. And the rioters, Luxemburgists I suppose, did not want to let me through." Lang paused, until he got a sign—raised eyebrows—that he'd secured his companion's attention.

"I said to the armed Communist rebels, 'It will take more than a revolution to stop me from directing!' Somehow, eventually, they understood. I must have been quite forceful when I was young."

Nebenzal said, *"Halfbreed."* Lang watched his face, in the oblique wash of passing streetlamps, and lit a cigarette. "The one about the Indian prince?"

"You've seen it," said Lang, waving his hand in front

of him, as if fending off fumes, a gesture he hoped would be read as modesty.

The car stopped for a light.

Nebenzal placed a hand on Lang's knee.

"Dumb bastard," he said to Lang.

The car started up, just as the light went green.

Lang extinguished his Boyard. Pulling Nebenzal close, so that Hugenberg's driver could not possibly overhear, Lang told the producer of his conversation with Pfeiffer. He spoke in his lowest voice, directly into Nebenzal's ear. He recounted verbatim Dr. Goebbels's objections to the manner of Mabuse's demise. He was close enough to smell Nebenzal's skin—Jew skin, scented with rosewater.

After a while, Nebenzal said, "Everyone's in show business," without smiling. Lang leaned back. Then, fishing the pouch of his gums with a forefinger, Lang found a small fragment of silvery amalgam which had somehow escaped his notice until now.

T H R E E

AN EARLY FOG HAVING LIFTED, THE TWO-engine plane left Tempelhof Airfield just past noon. The slight delay, the steward informed his passengers, would be made up, in entirety, by Koblenz. Thea had chosen a window seat, hopelessly addicted to the sight, from the air, of a receding Berlin; but condensation made it impossible to see anything save an intense halated white. Water, channeled by the plane's corrugated metal body, sluiced across the window in regular horizontal strips. She turned her attention to Sam, asleep now, open-mouthed, in the seat to her left.

An English edition of Sax Rohmer's *The Bride of Fu-Manchu* was splayed across his lap, spine up. Two fingers of Sam's left hand were curled around the buckram binding. (He'd gotten about a third of the way through, before dozing off.) Now the Lufthansa D-2600 hit an air pocket. Sam's head lolled back against the quilted leather seat, and he readjusted his grip on the Rohmer; but there was no break in his respiration's stately rasp. They had not gotten much sleep the night before. Thea had left Breitenbachplatz at midnight, picking Sam up at the Café Zuntz. They went on to the Romanische, where they'd had too much brandy; and back at Sam's hotel found themselves unable to sleep, finally drifting off near dawn.

Thea regarded, now, her sleeping companion, and decided it best to let him wake of his own accord. There was a bitter, slushy taste in her mouth. She took her eyes from the circle of stubble around Sam's open lips, at which she had yet to tire of looking, and flipped idly through *Die Dame*, which Lang in a fit of guilt had bought her three nights ago, and left on the foyer table. Marlene Dietrich was on the cover, but the story inside had little to do with her.

"Frau Lang," said the steward. It was her legal name, which gave her no pleasure. "Would you care for some coffee?" He wore a blue serge suit with much metallic braiding. His hair was cut brutally close at the neck, and Thea could see old acne scars, which a longer style would have concealed.

"Yes, please."

Sam, by all appearances dead to the world, lifted two fingers. Outside the rectangular window, the diffuse whiteness had become, if possible, brighter.

"Your companion has a wonderful tie," Ilsa Becker was saying from her seat across the aisle. "Quite unique." The Beckers lived in Stuttgart, socialized in Berlin; Thea knew Ilsa casually, from gallery openings, and from the opera. A week ago she had called to invite Thea to Nürburgring for the 1,000-kilometer auto race. Thea had promptly forgotten the invitation until last night at the Romanische when they'd run into Ilsa, who asked whether she should pick them up on her way to Tempelhof. Her husband Walter, she explained, was already at the ring, which was why she was being so sinful, staying up after hours, eating a soft-boiled egg in a glass.

The plane abruptly rose, then sank.

"I have not seen another like it," Ilsa went on now. Sam's tie, which he wore outside a dun shawl-collar sweater, featured a nude woman, one arm modestly concealing a breast. Above and below in painted lower-case script, a legend read:

je ne vois pas la

cachée dans la forêt

"What does it say?" Ilsa was asking.

"I do not see the woman hidden in the forest," Sam replied without opening his eyes, in a German which was slow but surprisingly well accented. He'd been in Germany two years, on and off, Paris before that. He told Thea, when they met, that he was from the Brooklyn section of New York City; but his passport said Philadelphia, and the postmark on the thin airmail envelopes, which bore news from home and the monthly check, was Bala-Cynwyd, Pennsylvania.

"I didn't know he was awake," said Ilsa.

Thea knew it annoyed him when her friends referred to him in the third person; but if it was bothering him, he was not showing it now. He was thirteen years younger than Thea. Ilsa, who'd been introduced to him twice, seemed not to have caught his name. Once, when Thea had dragged him to the ballet, several of her woman friends gave Sam long, appraising regard, as if he were something divine she had just brought home from the costume jeweler's. She did not explain to them that Sam filed dispatches with *Agence France-Presse*, cultural things for the most part, on a free-lance basis. Often he'd go out

6 3

with his Ciné-Kodak 16, bringing back footage which he'd sell to the newsreels. She recalled him packing the camera earlier that morning, and wondered how much time he'd spend, at the race, obtaining footage of the actualities.

The steward set down cups, half full against turbulence, in front of them. Sam lifted his eyelids partway. His eyes, it seemed to her, were the same color as the coffee, and the obscure correspondence between half-filled cups, half-opened eyes, caused her to smile. The engines were vibrating in subtly varying rhythms, cresting every fifteen seconds or so. The sky seemed to brighten and darken in sympathy with the pulse of engines. Thea leaned back in her seat, allowing the noise to wash over her.

"Fräulein von Harbou?" It was the man in the window seat to Ilsa's left. He was thin, with a scar which ran from his eye to the corner of his mouth. "I have a great admiration for your work." Thea nodded thanks. "I write for the *Tageblatt*," he went on. "I'm Anton Seitz."

"Pleased," Thea told him. She did not extend her hand, which would have had to reach across Sam, the aisle, and Ilsa to meet his.

Seitz said, "Do you find it hard getting ideas?"

"No."

"You enjoy writing, then?"

"Oh yes."

"Would you say your work has a particular theme?"

Thea sipped at her coffee, simultaneously weak and bitter. "The inexorability," she replied, "with which the first guilt entails the last atonement."

Seitz compressed his lips. Ilsa was nodding gravely. Thea took the opportunity to say, "Excuse," allowing her head to rest against Sam's wooly shoulder. The waves of engine noise were coming more rapidly now, and the seat fell away abruptly as they hit another spot of turbulence. Thea felt her stomach drop with it. The sky outside was a dismaying off-white now, almost greenish. She looked at the *Fu-Manchu* book on Sam's lap. Many of her early scenarios had dealt with Oriental themes as well: UFA thought audiences drawn to exotic locales. Now Thea wanted to do something Eastern once more, but in a serious way, not a costume drama like *Destiny*. Then the D-2600 dropped again, and she could no longer hold her eyes to the cabin interior. Seitz seemed to be droning on, to Ilsa, about auto racing, about the bygone days of the great factory teams. "Mercedes," he was saying, "with the blond mountain goat Stuck, the inimitable von Brauchitsch, Lautenberg, Sailer, Salzer, Werner, the great bear Merz, names which ring like a litany of German racing greatness. Or the Bugatti team, pride of France, with the smiling Chirion—"

Thea pressed her knuckles against her eyelids until explosions of rhodopsin purple spread out like clouds against the black. She tried to invoke onion towers, minarets; and tried, by a similar alchemy, to transform the throb of Lufthansa engines into the haunting, half-heard wail of a muezzin, atop one of those minarets, sirocco-borne, across the Medina.

Thea von Harbou had been somewhat overweight in her thirties, but had trimmed down in the past few years; and now, at forty-four, was quite striking. Her carriage—as proper as that of her husband—together with the black Persian henna she applied to her hair, gave her the effect of one perhaps five years younger. The semicircles beneath each pale blue eye were quite dark, but it was difficult to tell at one glance whether to impute them to age, the occasion, or character.

She was born in Tauperlitz, Bavaria, in 1888, two days after Christmas. Her father, Theodor, was a game-keeper, who sent her to Luisen convent for her education. (There had been land in the family at one point, in Saxony; but the last of it had been sold off by Theodor's grandfather, a man with a predilection toward the crackpot investment.) Thea had an older and a younger brother, the former killed in the war, the latter a brat, now in Thuringia—married to a bovine type whom Thea avoided at family functions. Just last November Frederick and the cow had made her an aunt, a privilege which had cost her the price of a sterling porringer. Thea had received a thank-you note, ostensibly signed by the niece herself, praising Thea's thoughtfulness. Soon it would be Easter, she'd be seeing them again, and her sister-in-law would be telling Thea how much she loved "*Metropolis,* and all the others."

"—Carraciola, German's best," Seitz was going on, at the fringes of her hearing, "who would don a Mercedes as if his own skin, reduced to driving the laughable Alfa! The only reason to even bother thinking about racing now? That audacious Mantuan, Nuvolari, champion of all Italy." His voice lapped in and out, as he explained to Ilsa that Nürburgring was an amalgam of corners bound to-gether by straights too short to mention. "Give the Mantuan a corner, and watch him hurtle around it faster than any man on earth—"

Thea had begun to write while still at the university, and her stories were bought up by popular journals almost immediately. (Looking through them last Christmas, at her father's house, she'd been embarrassed; "The Way in the Night" and "The Silent Pond" were laced with a precocious world-weariness which did not age well. She tried to recall how much Goethe she'd been reading at the time. Still, there were parts of "The Candle," two decades old, which did not displease her.) At twenty-three, overcome by patriotism, Thea began writing stories all of which, it seemed to her now, had been entitled "Beloved Fatherland," or perhaps "The Flag." Her first novel, *The Flight of Beate Hoyermann*, came two years later, and was the first work she'd not gone through a period of disowning. Then came the marriage to Klein-Rogge. Though she'd been in no sense a housewife—and though she could not recall any conscious thought to put writing aside—somehow nothing got finished those four years. Then she was twenty-nine. Thea recalled no decision to leave Rudolf, or to recommence the work; somehow though, by thirty, Klein-Rogge was gone and she was writing again. She once told Lang that she'd been quite sad, and had written her way out of it, which seemed as good a way as any of describ-ing it.

When she began to work again she took up screenplays for Joe May, things she could turn out quickly, and which paid well enough for her to live independently. The second one was *The Wandering Image*, on which she collaborated with the film's director, Fritz Lang. (Thea preferred her original title, *Madonna of the Snow*.) They worked together again on *Fighting Hearts*, a vehicle for Carla Trolle and Klein-Rogge which the studio insisted on releasing as *Four Around a Woman*. It was not until 1922, after *Destiny* and *Mabuse*, that the rumors surrounding the death of Lang's first wife seemed to lose currency, and they felt free to wed.

Since then she had written the scenarios for all of Lang's films: the two parts of the *Nibelungen* saga, of which she preferred the enchanted romance of *Siegfried's Death* to the fireworks of *Kriemhild's Revenge*; *Metropolis*, her favorite; *Spies*, with Klein-Rogge once more as an evil mastermind; the science-fiction epic *Woman in the Moon*; their first sound film, *M*; and now the just completed *Testament*. In the twenties she'd written scenarios for Dreyer, Dupont, and Murnau as well. Somehow she had also found time to make novels out of *The Hindu Tomb* and *Metropolis*, as well as to write *Spies*, upon which her later scenario was based. (*Spies* was pulp melodrama, not unlike Sam's beloved *Fu-Manchu*. Sam had been reading the Fu-Manchu novels, one after the other, for months now. Thea had read her first one, *Return of Fu-Manchu*, over Sam's shoulder, by gas fire in the Hotel vom Epoch—two weeks after they'd met, just before he left for Spain, she for Christmas in Tauperlitz. Two months ago, when they had been happy.) She had not shown Sam her earlier fiction, feeling it too German; and she kept from him *You're Impossible, Joe!*, a serious novel she'd done three years ago. Her publisher had introduced it to the bookstores clandestinely, and even those who had been able to find the thing seemed not to have liked it.

"You must promise not to quote me," Ilsa was saying to the reporter.

"Word of honor."

"The Chancellor called Dr. Kissel personally, and told him to get Mercedes back in the racing business. It is a priority for the new government, and the Chancellor says money is no longer an issue."

Thea opened her eyes. The light outside the window had gone bulging, ominous; and Thea thought how horrible it would be to be hit by lightning, sudden turbulence, found days later, bodies and wreckage strewn over acres of Eifel mountains. Charred remains. Limbs outflung at awkward, broken angles. The stench of fuel oil, burnt flesh. She would wire Lang, from the airport, to let him know she'd be away for a night or two; and perhaps wire the deskman separately, instructing him to put a fresh rose in the foyer vase.

"May I have your fullest attention please," the steward with acne was saying, standing at the front of the craft, arms behind him. "The density of precipitation over Koblenz precludes, for the moment, our use of it as a landing site." He rocked back and forth on his heels. "We will be setting down at Trier, and we will get you to Koblenz, rest assured, free of additional surcharge."

The passengers groaned on cue. Seitz was explaining to Ilsa that rain would cause Alfas and Bugattis to spin out at velocities which would cause no problem for a far heavier Mercedes.

" 'Mussolini so far has eluded me,' " said Sam abruptly. His eyes were open now. " 'But President Hoover, who stood in my path, makes way for Franklin Roosevelt. Mustapha Pasha is a regrettable nuisance, but my organization in Anatolia neutralizes his influence—' " She looked at him. The steward was between him and Ilsa now, and she doubted whether Sam could be overheard.

" 'I have tried to forget King Carol—but negligible quantities can upset the nicest equation,' " he went on, more loudly now. Thea watched him as he glanced down

69

to the Rohmer book, now face up on his lap. Then he continued, augmenting his speech with outsized hand and arm movements. " 'A man ruled by women is always dangerous, unless the women are under my orders.' " The engines were throbbing loudly, but there was little chance Ilsa could fail to overhear.

" 'Rumania, the oboe of the Balkan orchestra!' " Sam fell back, arching his throat, palms upward on the knees, as if drained by the very thought.

"Please prepare for landing," the steward was saying. Ilsa was asking how late they would be, by the time they finally got to Koblenz; and the steward was responding that Adenau—where the ring was located—was no farther from Trier than from Koblenz.

Ilsa said, "But my husband was to have picked us up in Koblenz."

"I'm sure he will await you there," said the steward, left hand in pocket.

"Oh," Ilsa said.

"We'll have lunch," Thea told Ilsa, when it was clear her companion was at a loss. "We'll cable Walter, have him pick us up in Trier."

Seitz was going on about the lightweight Bugattis, which could with luck go the whole race without a tire change, while Mercedes lost valuable seconds in the pit. Weak green light penetrated the rectangular windows, suffused the cabin, rendering ugly the faces of those inside. Sam, spent after his outburst, was once more asleep. She would thumb through the *Fu-Manchu* later, find the passage from which Sam had been so vocally quoting. "Soon all Germany will know," Ilsa was telling the reporter with the handsome scar, "that the Chancellor is a great auto-racing enthusiast."

Then, to the accompaniment of many sickening lurches, the windows went white once more, pale glare overfilling the interior, obliterating all detail. Thea closed her eyes. Ilsa was conferring with the steward, demanding use of the airport telephone and wire facilities to alert her husband—at Koblenz, in Adenau, at the track, wherever he might be—that his wife awaited. Thea did not know what she was doing aboard this plane, en route to an event for which she had little affinity. It occurred to her that Sam and Lang were both, in different ways, filmmakers; and she wondered why this had not, for some reason, occurred to her long before. Then they were on the ground, braking harshly so as not to overshoot the provincial airstrip. As the reporter Seitz bent forward to reach his coat, Thea caught momentary sight of the butt of an automatic pistol, protruding from a weblike leather strap device beneath his left armpit. It seemed strange that a reporter for the *Tageblatt*, which was liberal, and owned by Jews, would be carrying a gun, like some common thug. Sensing the plane to have rolled to a stop, Sam stood up, opened his eyes.

Thea and Ilsa had taken the cable car from Zurlauben harbor. It had ascended obliquely across the Mosel; and in eight minutes they were at the Weisshaus, whose restaurant deck, enclosed by huge sheets of outward-slanting windows, afforded a wide-angle view of the river and of Trier beyond. Ilsa, who during adolescence had spent several months in the Trier with an aunt, now gave Thea her gloss on the view below. The palace gardens, whose formally arrayed pools and flower beds could be seen to best advantage from this height; Porta Nigra, a double arcade Ilsa held to be "the finest Roman relic in Germany"; and between them, the Church of Our Lady, early Gothic, nearly circular. Its bizarre proportions suggested to Thea the onion tower she'd seen, with her eyes closed, on the airplane. Every vista, Thea thought now, should have a gateway, a church, a garden, a river. The air outside the double-glazed window was thin, surprisingly clear. Flecks of light bounced off the Mosel, as if the river were a gilded cordon, holding the tourist at decent length from the treasures on the far bank. If she were designing the view, Thea thought, the garden would be in the center, with church and gate on either side; and perhaps another river, visible only on the most beautiful of days, lending protective symmetry to the far side of the panorama. Thea was certain, now, that she'd seen the *Tageblatt* reporter somewhere before, though just where was beyond her present grasp.

"I've had worse veal," Ilsa announced. Thea looked up to see Ilsa patting her lips with a folded dinner napkin. Sam had stayed in town, saying he'd rather walk around than eat. (She supposed he needed respite from the company of women.) They were to rendezvous on Kaiserstrasse, by the entrance to the imperial baths, at five, where Herr Becker would pick them up. "Where did they find fresh grapes," Ilsa was asking, "this time of year?"

"Flown in, I suppose." Thea wished she had saved some of her husband's cocaine, from Wednesday night, because she was fading, and it would certainly be useful now. But there was no way she could have asked for some to take with her. She looked out once more to the palace gardens. Sam could be there now, miming hide-and-seek, dodging Belgian tourists among files of topiary hedgework. "And the fish?" Ilsa was asking.

"Decent." Thea would have preferred to have the veal as well. She was in no sense a practicing Catholic anymore, but still could not bring herself to eat meat on Friday.

Ilsa said, "Should I have an affair?" Sun glared off the oriels of the church, gilding perhaps a third of them, on the left. She could not look at them intently for any length of time.

"Do you have anyone in mind?" Thea said finally. She realized, after she responded, that this was probably Ilsa's way of asking how Thea managed, with husband and lover. It was not something Thea wanted to discuss with her.

"Short. Dark. Swarthy. If it has to be an Italian, so be it." Ilsa laughed, patted her mouth once more, signaled the waiter. "Besides," she went on, "Walter has his cars to play with." It was warm, and Thea wondered whether the few centimeters of dead air, between inner and outer panes, could be held responsible for the lack of condensation on the windows. After *Testament* was released, and things settled down, she would see if she felt like writing another scenario for Lang. There was the Oriental story, but it was not, for some reason, a story she thought Lang could best realize. There was really no need, she told herself, to think about these things now. She was, in a sense, on vacation.

"It will be so good for Walter," Ilsa went on, "that Mercedes will be racing again."

"Yes," Thea heard herself say. She looked across to the cable car. It was again in motion, one car descending, one climbing, the two abreast of one another for several instants now, above the Mosel. Suppose the archfiend and his crew were descending, the hapless prosecutor von Wenk still on his way up. The two could exchange shots across that narrow gap. Perhaps one of the archfiend's henchmen, pulling some huge lever, had stalled the machinery, leaving the prosecutor dangling prey for the battalion of miscreants in the adjacent cab. What to do, about the innocent bystanders? Would they panic? Would the prosecutor lose precious seconds, engaged in their reassurance?

Ilsa was inserting an earring. "You are so lucky, dear Thea, to have a man without a mustache!" Thea assumed she was referring to Sam, although Lang had not yet succumbed to that prerogative of masculine success. She recalled in fact having noticed Wednesday night that Lang was the only male guest without one. Hugenberg's ludicrous soup strainer had bobbed up and down as he'd grandstanded at some length about the need for the responsible right wing to ensure that elections not be suspended. He went on about the threat from Communists, and Anarchists, such as those who had set fire to the Reichstag; and gave his approval, as if anyone were waiting for it, to the proclamation suspending civil liberties, and the illegalization of the Communist party. "But," he'd added, in his best stentorian tone, "nothing must prejudice my party's chance at victory in Monday's elections!" Thea had waited an additional quarter hour after he'd finished before excusing herself, lest her departure be ascribed to politics. Lang had known, for hours, that she'd be leaving separately; but when she glanced back, he was wearing his sick-dog look, eyes gone large with yearning, as if he'd been hoping all the while she'd stay. Thea could see now that the archfiend would extend grappling hooks, pulling the prosecutor's cab perilously off axis. Someone would end up in the drink.

"I think I shall take a lover," Ilsa was saying, her hand on Thea's forearm.

"If you wish." Thea looked down once more to the topiary gardens, whose crosshatched mazes she'd imaged Sam to be wandering. The sight recalled for her the Pigeon Board, a large wall in the Alexanderplatz police station covered floor to ceiling with a gridded map of Berlin. (They had shown it to her while she was researching police procedure, for M.) Along the window opposite the map ran a room-length row of pigeon stalls, numbered serially. Two hundred undercover policemen, Commander Friedrich explained, were stationed at precise locations. Each bore an innocent-appearing package containing a homing pigeon. Catching sight of the suspect, the officer surreptitiously released his bird, which would home to its specific coop. Upon the arrival of a pigeon in, say, stall 154, one of Friedrich's men would place a yellow pin at the appropriate spot on the grid. (One fifty-four, she recalled for some reason, was Bülowstrasse.) "The pigeons," the commander had declaimed, "remained unmarked, lest they fall into enemy hands. Yet, with this system, our men can report to base without losing sight of the quarry, or arousing undue suspicion." Thea wondered just whose movements were being described by that succession of yellow pins on the gridded Pigeon Board now; and what Commander Friedrich's men did, when the fugitive escaped the grid's confines, beyond the limits of Berlin.

Ilsa was running her finger down the column of numbers on the check. "This seems correct," she said, and then, after a pause, "I shall take this one."

"I thank you," Thea heard herself say.

Ilsa said, "Should I set my cap for an audacious Mantuan?"

The room at Adenauer Hof faced east; Thea had forgotten to close the shutters, and thin, painfully slanting light woke her just past dawn. Sam's head was turned away from her, and it was impossible to tell from his breathing whether he were on this side of wakefulness or the other. They'd been to a horrid party in the hotel "ballroom" the night before, and now she was awake at the same hour that, just a day ago, she'd been settling down to sleep. Somewhere in the intervening day and night there had been a plane trip, two bouts of cable car, several automobile tours.

Sam lifted the pillow. He said, "Good morning," in a surprisingly civil voice, before replacing the pillow over his head. Unguided by sight, his hand poked out from beneath the blankets, felt its way to the night table, where it seized the open pack of Camels. He'd gotten what the night clerk claimed to be the last two packs in all Adenau. (Thea had never seen him go without.)

"Shall we order up breakfast?" she asked, trying out her voice.

He sat up, two pillows behind him now, cigarette dangling from his thick lips. It was the way she wanted to remember him. At length she rose, slipped a wrapper over her nightgown. At the window she looked down upon a seemingly endless procession of autocars and bicycles on the road which twisted upward, toward the ring. Sam, coming up from behind, pressed himself to her.

"There must be several thousand," he said finally.

Thea watched the cyclists navigate the channel between two lanes of nearly motionless autocars. She said, "It must be quicker to walk." The line of cars extended to the near hills where it was enveloped by mist. It was not, she told herself, a bad vista. At the party the night before Thea had been set upon by a pair of provincial academics, Rhinelanders, purveyors of stupefaction. They'd gone on about the scenery, and Sam, muttering a few words in French, had excused himself. She could not recall an instance of Sam doing anything he did not want to. "It's not yet seven," he was saying now, from the far side of the room. "Where did you hide my shirt?"

Thea asked, "What time does the race start?" She turned to watch him in his sleeveless undershirt which made him look, she fancied, like a Chicago gangster. He rummaged in his suitcase. Thea wondered why men did up their trousers fully, knowing full well they'd only have to undo all those buttons, seconds later, to tuck in the shirt.

"Where did you hide it?" Sam was saying.

Thea sat at the writing desk, pushing aside two picture postcards Sam had written last night. They were addressed to André Breton and Yves Tanguy, in Paris. She tried to recall the details of a story Sam had told her, early on, about a riot they had staged in a restaurant. Breton had become enraged, apparently, at finding that someone had dared open a chic bistro called Maldoror. Breton, Sam, six or seven others, attacked the restaurant on Valentine's Day, avenging the appropriation of a name the Surrealists regarded as belonging to themselves. She studied the postcards now, idealized photos of the view from Adenau's main square. Sam, like Lang, wrote only just before retiring. Thea had often seen Sam address postcards to his notorious Paris friends; but she could not recall seeing, among his effects at the vom Epoch, any correspondence from them.

"I don't have your shirt." The sun was rising on a darkening sky. At the window once more, Thea tried to make out the exact point where the line of automobiles became lost to the fog. The cars were not moving now, or moving only occasionally; and in two or three spots drivers were standing by the side of their autos, warming hands over small impromptu bonfires.

" 'Let me tell you of Carraciola and Nuvolari,' " Sam began in recitative monotone. " 'A great tale of racing's unwritten rule. Last year, at Monaco, the both of them driving the type 8-C Monza—' " Sam had spent a good deal of time at last night's party with the *Tageblatt* reporter, who was regaling him and Ilsa with car lore. She had watched Sam stare off into the middle distance, distractedly taking it in. Thea supposed now she was still angry that he'd abandoned her with the academics. They reminded her of people she had known in Tauperlitz, and of what she might have become, perhaps, had she not written her way out. She wondered how long the work on the house at Dahlem would take. The hounds could not be very happy, in boarding. Thea crossed to the bed and grabbed a pillow.

" 'Don't confuse,' " Sam was going on, " 'Monza, the track with Monza, the car.' How will you explain the feathers, strewn all over this room, to the chambermaid? I'm talking about Monza the car, the type 8-C."

Thea, who had been holding the pillow a short distance above Sam's head, let go. It fell, seeming for a moment as if it would balance atop his head. Then it slid, off his neck onto the bed.

"You are such a boy," Thea told him.

He spent a moment looking hurt before recomposing his features. His "hurt" look was nearly identical to the expression Lang used for such occasions. Thea switched on the overhead electrolier; then, finding it too bright, switched it off. Sam, at the phone, was telling Room Service he wanted juice, coffee, croissants, for two. Thea watched him for a while, then lay down on the other side of the bed.

"The race starts at half-past nine," he said.

"Boys. Boys and their cars." Thea took a cigarette from Sam's pack, lit it. She could not be bothered with the holder. There was a blare of car horns outside the window. Turning on her side, she extended her arm, playing with the curls behind his ear. "Will they race, even in the rain?" she asked softly. There was a knock at the door.

"Oh yes," said Sam.

The knocking came again.

"It's open," Thea yelled, somewhat too loudly.

The bellhop wore a V-shaped tunic, heroically wide at the shoulder. It was emblazoned with horizontal metallic stripes of decreasing length. He held in front of him a silver tray, which bore a business-size buff-colored envelope. Sam turned away as Thea took the envelope with her name, found change for the tip.

"Where did they find the uniform?" asked Sam after the bellhop had left. "A walking glockenspiel. The man who found me a pack of Camels, last night, was wearing a hat that actually came to a point on top. You could have turned him upside down," he went on rapidly, "and used him to pick up scraps of paper in the park."

Thea held the envelope, gazing at the wire-service insignia on the back flap.

Sam said, "I guess I was expecting coffee." He went to his suitcase, extracted the Ciné-Kodak. It was rectangular, with rounded corners, not too big to be held with two hands. Its surface with wrinkle-finish black, with chrome edging. The windup key folded flat against its side. Next to the lens, in English, were settings for Dull Days or in Open Shade; Bright Days to Slightly Cloudy; Direct Sunlight; Intensely Bright. Each had its own F-stop number.

"I'll read it later."

"Don't be silly," said Sam over the blare of car horns, much louder now. Still holding the camera he walked toward the bathroom, closing the door fully behind him. There was a thin strip of light at the bottom of the door, which went out. Thea opened the envelope.

> AM WRITING NEW SCREENPLAY,
> SOLO STOP ALL MY LOVE TO
> YOU STOP YOUR FRITZ

When she got back to Berlin she would have to ask him just why he'd found it necessary to inform her, by wire, that he was sitting at the typewriter. He would respond,

Thea knew, offhandedly, saying he simply assumed she would want to know.

"Oh. My shirt was in here!" said Sam from the bathroom. She heard metallic clicking noises, wondered if he were loading the Ciné-Kodak. Perhaps the telegram was Lang's way of letting her know what he could not bring himself to tell her: that he was seeing Lily again. Thea compressed her lips. Perhaps she should send a return wire, telling him that she had a vague idea for a screenplay, something Eastern, with minarets and onion towers.

"Frau Lang?"

The knocking at the door began again. Thea opened the door and a bellhop—different face, same tunic—wheeled in breakfast. Thea smiled, as he tipped his pointed hat in parting.

"I smell croissants." Sam emerged from the bathroom, camera in hand, clean-shaven. The shower was still running in the bathroom. He shut the door behind him. Outside the window a line of cyclists worked uphill, in the gutter between two lanes of stalled autos. She wondered if he was steaming the wrinkles from yesterday's shirt.

Thea said, "How will we get there?"

"I assume we walk. Let us leave the logistics to Herr Becker." The Beckers were to pick them up at eight.

"Let us eat," said Thea without enthusiasm.

Sam kissed the side of her neck, and said, "Lang?"

"Yes," she said. She fixed the chairs, and brought the table to the window. "It's all right," she told him.

"Everything's okay then?"

Thea toyed with her Countess Told cigarette holder. "I suppose so."

"I believe," said Sam, sitting down to breakfast, "I was speaking of the Monte Carlo. Carraciola racing an Alfa, the Monza 8-C, on his own, not as part of the Alfa team. Nuvolari took the lead from the start, setting a pace that was almost murderous on the long, twisting course." Sam buttered his croissant clumsily, small flaky pieces all down the front of his undershirt. She wanted to tell him to go riot in a restaurant, or whatever one did to pass the time in Paris, when one did not have to work for a living. "With each lap he worked his way forward, until nearly abreast of the Mantuan." He went on, about the unwritten rule of auto racing, which holds that among drivers of the same team, there is no competition: the one ahead at halftime drives home to victory. "During the last lap Nuvolari came so close Carraciola could look into the Mantuan's eyes. They were side by side, almost wheel to wheel. He watched as Nuvolari's fuel line fouled. Then came the finish line. Nuvolari drove through first, barely half speed. Carraciola, his foot off the accelerator, right behind."

The honking of horns outside had not abated. Where were Walter and Ilsa? Surely it was past eight now. There was a speck of jam on the left side of his nose. Thea thought about dipping her napkin into the water glass, wiping the speck away; but she did not.

"Carraciola was not part of the team. They had rejected him. He had no obligations to the Alfa people." Sam downed his juice in one long gulp, wincing a bit, as if it were straight whiskey.

He put the glass down and looked at Thea, the corners of his mouth going fractionally up and down. "Do you want me to leave?" he asked her.

Thea's stomach went away, as if she were back on the airplane, hitting turbulence. She could not believe that Sam was offering to bow out, ceding victory to Lang. Once again, Thea felt herself part of a complicated masculine exchange, herself the bartered gift. Then the wave of nausea passed.

Sam continued to look at her, eyelids half lowered.

"What did the crowd think?" Thea said finally.

"Jeers of contempt from the spectators," Sam replied immediately, grinning now, enormously pleased that she had asked. "They felt betrayed."

Thea said, "Oh." Somehow, obscurely, Thea had always felt that writing novels and films would protect her from moments like this; and could only think now that she'd not written them well enough. Sam was at the window, making a show of lighting a Camel. She could tell that he wanted her to say something.

"Where would you go, Sam. Brooklyn?"

He propped his left foot on the radiator. "I would be lost," he said, making grand, expansive movements with the Camel, "without you." The cigarette's lighted tip left a brief trail of afterimage behind it, against the gray sky outside.

"Ask me to dance," Sam said, proffering his arms. "February twenty-ninth. Leap Year's day. The women ask the men. You do that," he exhaled, "in Germany?" Thea did not tell him that it was the fourth of March and not, in any case, a leap year. Soon she would be watching a pack of boys, in small colored machines, whizzing round and round under falling rain. Perhaps writing was not enough. Someday they would let her direct films, and she would have control over her destiny.

"Dance with me," Thea heard herself say. She would give Walter and Ilsa another minute, then would call them if they did not show. Sam was at the radio cabinet now. There was the tail end of a news broadcast. Thalmann, head of the Communist party, which had been outlawed Tuesday in the wake of the Reichstag fire, had been arrested. Torgler had given up. They were still looking for Dimitroff. Sam waited a bit for more news; then, hearing only a chocolate advertisement, spun the dial, stopping at a waltz. It was Viennese-sounding, unfamiliar to Thea. Sam's arms were once more extended in invitation. Thea placed her chin in the hollow of Sam's neck and could smell his aftershave, which he mixed himself, from witch hazel and bay rum, as he made to lead her about the hotel-room floor.

Thea pressed herself to him. She closed her eyes. There was a knock at the door and they stopped dancing. They clung to each other for several moments, Thea's hand, beneath the American undershirt, urgently working the muscles of Sam's back.

She had seen the Pigeon Board, and knew its map to end at the outskirts of Berlin; but perhaps there was another room, whose wall was covered with a map of all the world. It would be on this map that the yellow pins would have been inserted, quite close together, as she had swirled about the floor. She was not sure, but thought now that it had been in Alexanderplatz, in one of the rooms reserved for Friedrich's secret police, that she had first seen the man with the thin whitish scar, who had, on the plane, introduced himself as a newspaper reporter, and who last night had been so effusive, with stories of automobiles and the men who drive them.

There was a flash of lightning outside, which could be heard as static on the radio. Then Thea was listening to the Viennese waltz once more, and Ilsa's voice—calling her name from the other side of the wooden door—in the abrupt interval before the thunderclap. The center of the storm must not be far. Thea told herself to remember to count the seconds, next time lightning flashed.

F O U R

THE FLASH BARS WENT OFF AGAIN, LIKE AN
expressionist thunderstorm, casting stark elongated shadows on the wall of the pit. Kautz wore a tan single-breasted
raincoat. Merz had a similar raincoat, draped over his
shoulders. Von Brauchitsch was seated between them. He
had an olive drab double-breasted coat which he wore, like
Merz, without putting his arms through the sleeves. Their
faces were whited out again, and again; then one of them
smiled, and the bloom of light seemed continuous. All
three were in white belted racing suits, with zippered
breast pockets, and protective goggles, which hung loosely
now about their necks. Merz and von Brauchitsch slicked
their hair straight back. Kautz wore a part just one side of
center. The room seemed to shudder as flashes were thrown
off at odd, differing angles. Kautz rolled his eyes and was
shot a dirty look by Alfred Neubauer, the Mercedes racing
manager, who had been supervising the photo session.
"Just a bit more," he said quietly. Merz fingered the band
of his white racing cap.

"That's it," Neubauer said.

The flashes became more intermittent. Two men,
Neubauer's assistants, herded groaning photographers back
toward the press area. Thea noticed a woman with dyed
black hair not unlike her own, familiar from somewhere,

holding a small movie camera. Neubauer's assistants were saying, "No questions!" over and over.

"Ilsa," Neubauer said, doffing his hat. He was wearing a three-piece suit with lapels on the vest, a wide silk tie, and a raincoat much like those of Kautz and Merz, though larger, accommodating his bulk.

"May I present Thea von Harbou? Thea, this is Alfred Neubauer."

"Charmed." Thea was glad that Ilsa had not introduced her as Frau Lang. Sam had gotten halfway to the track before he realized he had forgotten his camera, and gone back to retrieve it. He'd missed the photo session, and would probably miss the checkered flag.

"The pleasure," said Neubauer, "is mine." He turned toward the track, then stopped when Ilsa made to follow him.

"Let me arrange seats for you in the press section." Neubauer tugged at an earlobe. His hair was cut quite short, no more than a stubble.

Ilsa said, "Walter told us—"

"Be assured it's nothing personal. Drivers are quite superstitious. They will not race, for instance, if peanut shells have been found in the pit area. We're all modern, and were the decision mine I would let women watch from trackside. Fräulein von Harbou. It is indeed an honor. 'Beloved Fatherland' is one of my very favorite stories."

Thea smiled. "Thank you," she said.

They walked up a ramp of badly nailed wooden slats which led toward the roped-in area, with folding chairs, assigned to the press. Neubauer assured Ilsa he would send her love to Walter.

"Until victory," Thea told him.

"You take care of these women," he said to the tieless man who inspected credentials.

"Kautz looks so young, so worried," Ilsa was saying. "I'd much prefer him to Merz, who is far too beefy, though Walter says he can hammer a nail barehanded." Thea looked up toward the green canvas canopy held up, quite tenuously it seemed, by guy ropes attached to the speaker columns. She had stuffed some money into Sam's breast pocket, telling him to remember his hip flask, and to fill it with something first-rate. (Sam didn't really have need of the money; but Thea enjoyed the gesture. The feel of his shirt pocket, from the inside.) Below, on the track now, the cars were being pushed into position. They were shoving a blue one into place on the first starting row. It must be a Bugatti. The details of racing weren't something you couldn't pick up, in a day or two, with a bit of application.

"Anton said the rain would be good for Germany," Ilsa was saying.

"Yes." The woman with the movie camera was down on the track now, telling a tall man—one of her crew?—where to place his tripod, and what kind of framing she wanted from him. Thea wondered why she had been given permission to be on the track, where the fair sex were forbidden.

"Walter!" Ilsa screamed. Thea saw Ilsa's husband, a fair-skinned man with receding lank blond hair. He was supervising two other men, who were pushing a tan-colored Mercedes into the second row. The Mercedes looked huge, clumsy next to the Alfa and the Bugatti. Ilsa screamed again, and her husband waved back with both arms. Then he was wiping condensation from his wire-rim glasses. Track announcements poured from the speaker horns overhead. Thea could discern the first syllable or so of each phrase, the rest lost to multiple echo.

"Which one is Carraciola?" Ilsa was asking Seitz, the elegant, scarred *Tageblatt* reporter, now seated to Ilsa's right.

"Not racing today," he said, lowering binoculars. Thea felt a pair of hands over her eyes.

"Sam," Thea said.

"He was injured—" Seitz began.

Sam said, "I'll bet you thought I'd miss the flag," moving his hands to her shoulder. There was a squeaking sound as he maneuvered one of the folding wooden chairs beside her own. He sat down with drunken abruptness.

"—training for Monte Carlo."

Sam leaned forward, looking past Thea, past Ilsa. "Is he all right?" he asked, with an emphasis which was hard to read.

"It's doubtful," Seitz said, "whether he will be able to race again. Lucky if he walks, actually. Thigh pretty much shattered."

"I didn't know," said Ilsa, holding Seitz's forearm. Sam said, "Slivovitz," and passed the beaten silver flask to him. Thea could not help but smile at the thought of Sam, told to bring back something first-rate, returning drunkenly with Polish plum brandy, and terribly pleased with himself in the bargain. She recalled now that the *Tageblatt* was the paper in which *You're Impossible, Joe!* had received its only notice.

"Harrison, AFP," Sam said loudly, as if introducing himself. Most of the drivers were in their cars. Thea counted thirty-one. The engines were starting now. Their overlapping roar recalled for her the engines of the Lufthansa the day before. The announcements lost all intelligibility. The wind was blowing toward them now, and Thea wondered if they were far enough back to stay dry. The woman in coveralls still had access to the track.

"It's a pity," Ilsa was saying, "to leave such a man at the mercy of Italian doctors."

Seitz reseated his hat at a more jaunty angle. Thea had told Sam that she would be more comfortable, on public occasions, were he to wear a proper hat; but most of the time he showed up bareheaded, as now, or worse, in a cloth cap. "To put it another way, Frau Becker," the reporter was saying, "may I tell my readers that Mercedes is back in the racing business?"

"You would have to ask Walter."

Sam was taking another long swallow from the flask. She wondered what it meant that he was always forgetting things, and having to go back for them, or finding other reasons to be on his own for an hour. All the engines were started now. It was not possible to distinguish the sound of any one above the din. "Will Mercedes be producing small cars, for the new formula?" Seitz was shouting now.

Ilsa actually batted her eyelashes. She passed Thea the flask which Thea passed in turn to Sam, who drained it. Sam seemed suddenly quite pale.

"He would have found out soon enough anyway," Ilsa was saying, as if in rehearsal for a later talk with her husband. Sam was holding the Ciné-Kodak to his eye, sighting the track along its top edge.

"Are you all right?" Thea asked him, just loudly enough to be heard over all else. Now the camera was in his lap, and he was winding it. The spring-driven mechanism, he'd once told her, had a tendency to run down; and when projected, his footage would often speed up comically, toward the end of each shot, the sedate Sunday promenade breaking into a trot.

"I guessed as much," Seitz was saying, "from the Chancellor's speech three weeks ago at the auto show. His first nonpolitical speech as Chancellor." Thea looked behind her to the stands, just visible below the edge of the green canvas. The stands were full. It did not seem to bother them to be sitting in the rain. There were thousands of them.

"I'll be fine," Sam said finally.

" 'The railway is too impersonal, in that it restricts individual freedom.' " The reporter was reading from his notebook now. " 'It has required decades to realize the dream for a vehicle that would respond to the commands of the individual.' He goes on. 'The world is indebted to Daimler and Benz, German pioneer inventors, for the creation of a competitor to the railway. Today, the automobile and the airplane must be considered the most perfect instruments of transportation.' You know, the Chancellor refuses to travel by rail." Seitz dropped the notebook—black, Morocco bound—into his breast pocket.

"Walter was there. At the auto show," Ilsa was saying. Then the flag went down. There was a tremendous whoosh, and the cars were off, down the straightaway, around the first curve. Seitz's reading of the Chancellor's remarks seemed a bit reverential for a reporter from a Jewish paper. Thea became aware just how much of the noise was coming from the crowd in the stands behind her. She had been expecting, she supposed, a great whirl of dust in the wake, but the rain was falling quite hard now, and the cars left behind them only an eerie condensation, which clung low to the track bed.

Ilsa was looking out at the empty stretch of roadway. "How long," she asked finally, "before they come back?"

Anton Seitz said, "We shall see the leader reappear in twelve, thirteen minutes, depending."

Sam reached over, grabbed at Ilsa's shoulder. "As the race continues," he said in his carnival voice, the one he claimed to have learned when he ran away from home, to join the Brooklyn circus, "there will be more distance between the leader and the followers, and there will be something to watch for almost continuously."

Thea could not tell if Ilsa knew she was being mocked. Seitz was adjusting his tie.

"Or gaze intently, Ilsa, at the car you want to win. Then close your eyes, and do not reopen them, until that car is before us once more. Keep track of the images. And use them to construct a film of victory. Persistence of vision." Sam held the empty flask to his lips. "I'm all right," he said to Thea, breath metallic, plummy. "I haven't felt better in days."

"Just don't tell your readers," Ilsa was telling Seitz, "where you learned that we were tooling up."

"Today," Sam said loudly, "liquor constitutes the most perfect instrument of intoxication." Thea did not know how he could have gotten so drunk in so short a time. Breakfast had been minimal; but it should take far more than a 500-milliliter flask to get Sam this far along. She wondered if she would have to take him by the arm, and lead him into the path of an oncoming Bugatti. Perhaps she should send him off to someplace obscure,

high in the wet-wood stands, where he would cause neither
her embarrassment nor himself harm.

"It responds to the commands of the individual." He
brought the camera up, turned back and forth in his chair,
panning the spectacle. His finger was on the button, but
he seemed not to be pressing down.

"Keep them closed now," Sam shouted at Ilsa, who
stared ahead at empty track as if she did not hear him over
the roar.

"You should get some coffee into him. Some food,"
Ilsa whispered finally.

"The name is Sam," Sam said.

Thea said, "Let me get you—"

"That would just sober me up," he said, looking
straight at her.

Thea put her hand to her face. It was clammy with
condensation. She felt uncomfortable in her heavy black
wool coat but was sure she'd be far too cold without it.
Closing her eyes, she could see Lang at his desk, brow all
furrowed in a masque of creativity. The last thing he'd
written by himself was *Spiders*, fourteen years ago now:
unobjectionable serial pulp. She remembered now an in-
terview he'd given to *Filmworker*, in which he'd said that
in Thea he'd found "an invaluable assistant who out of
profound understanding of my intentions creates the manu-
scripts which became the basis of my work." He had
shown it to her, thinking she'd be pleased.

Ilsa said, "Von Brauchitsch," making a fist, moving it
a short distance laterally. There was a commotion in the
stands to their left. Seitz, consulting his pocket watch,
announced, "Another couple of minutes yet."

"If we know how fast the cars go, we don't know

where they are," Sam was saying, to no one in particular. "If we know where they are, we cannot tell how fast they go. Nobel Prizes are given for this." He ran fingers through his hair, letting his neck go slack. "I can't go on being charming," he told Thea quietly, eyes moist, half closed.

Thea said, "You haven't been charming for days."

"That's true." He gave out an exhausted smile, allowing his lids to fall all the way shut. Then he was out, his head on her shoulder, mouth open. A car sped by, then another, then several in a tight clump. There was something exciting, Thea found, about the pitch of the engines, all high and tense as they approached, thrillingly low as they sped by. It was the Doppler shift, something Lang had explained to her years ago.

"Mercedes! In the lead! I could tell!" Ilsa was applauding. Down in the boxes, Walter was making chalk marks on a slate. Thea craned her neck to get decent view of the thing.

BRAU

NUV

MERZ

FAG

As she shifted, Sam's head dropped neatly into her lap. Thea toyed absently with his hair, as Ilsa lit a cigarette for her. There were glistening tire tracks on the macadam which narrowed, as she watched, toward illegibility, as the rain filled them in.

"Are you voting tomorrow?" Ilsa was saying.

"I suppose so." Thea wondered whether the tire tracks

would disappear completely before the cars passed around again. "It would certainly be nice," she told Ilsa, "to put an end to all this *visiting*." It was a line she had picked up from that young Englishman, at the bad Italian restaurant where all the foreign journalists went. "The political situation here seems very dull," the fey young man had said. "Papen visits Hindenburg. Hitler visits Papen. Hitler and Papen visit Schleicher. Hugenberg pays a call on Hindenburg only to find him not at home." Thea smiling now, recalled Hugenberg, at Wednesday's dinner, describing his and Papen's latest contrivance, the red-white-black coalition. Now Seitz was explaining to Ilsa the new 750-kilogram formula, and the smaller, faster cars which would result. Sam began to snore audibly. It was time, Thea thought, to do something with an Eastern theme: something forlorn, mysterious, fated. Then noise went up from the left side of the stands, and the cars were coming around again. Thea tried to catch sight of Walter holding up the slate she'd watched him prepare, but there were too many people, in front of her, standing now. The cars, more spread out this time, took a good minute and a half to pass; and it was possible, for the first time, to distinguish the tone of the individual engine from the mass.

"Who leads?" Ilsa demanded.

"Brauchitsch," said Sam, in his sleep.

Rain was again rendering the tracks indistinct. Thea was able to pick out Walter, writing once more on the slate.

BRAU
NUV—12

She wondered whether Sam had discerned the leader by sound alone. Then he was standing, putting a lot of weight on the back of his wooden folding chair.

"Men's room," he said, enunciating quite clearly now.

"Let me walk you." The chair had started to tremble, and Thea took Sam's elbow.

They went down the ramp to the pit, the improvised bench along the far wall, where the photo session had been held. She wished she'd worn more sensible shoes than the lizard pumps. A wood plank led to a set of stairs which they mounted, Thea's arm around his waist, his head lolling slack and heavy on her shoulder.

They were up in the stands now, and the stairs—planks set too deeply for comfortable climbing—had become congested with fans. They had for the most part blank Rhinelander faces, and were heavier than Berliners. Thea could not believe the lack of separate facilities for press, and for guests in boxes. Directly ahead of her was a bulky woman carrying, on her shoulder, a small girl. The child, straight blonde hair cut in solemn bangs to just above the eyes, seemed for an instant quite beautiful; and Thea wondered how long before fate got a grip and she took on the bovine listlessness of her mother. Thea winked at the girl-child, who smiled conspiratorially over the back of her guardian. Thea took great pleasure in the stolen regard, as if the child knew, somehow—

"I'm fine," Sam said, taking his arm from her waist.

"Are you all right?" They were at a landing now, midway up the stands, and Sam fell in line with the queue of males, extending to a doorway perhaps ten meters down. They were no longer sheltered by the green canvas, below them now. The rain had become a fine mist. Thea walked with Sam as the line advanced. A stench of urine and disinfectant.

"I'm fine." He seemed embarrassed to be the only man there with a female companion.

"Meet me," said Thea, gesturing toward the staircase.

"Right."

There was a high whine, now abruptly lower, swallowed up by cheers and shouts. She watched the spectators in the front row stand up, and those in the rows behind them, until all were on their feet. More overlapped echoes from the loudspeakers. At the back several spectators sat down to await the next lap. She hoped Sam would not be long, and they could return to the press section, whose occupants were not quite so pungent of wet wool and sauerkraut. Then she heard the unmistakable double tone of an ambulance klaxon, down on the track. Three men in front of her stood at once, sat back down when it became clear there was nothing to be seen. She found that she had been thinking, for some time really, of her niece in Thuringia. The unsupported wooden flooring planks, nailed down at each end, were wet, and there was an uncomfortable play when Thea stepped upon them. She did not know what could be taking Sam so long.

A voice on the loudspeaker, abruptly intelligible: "We have just received information that Mercedes driver Merz has skidded off the course. He is said to be injured."

Thea looked around for the blonde child whom she'd winked at, over its mother's shoulder, moments ago. The last few syllables of the announcement could be heard again, bouncing multiply off hard surfaces. A man behind her and to her left began to scream. The woman with him was yelling as well. Then Sam was beside her, eyes wide, some color to his skin.

He said, "I didn't catch—"

The man's scream and the woman's yelling were lost to the larger noise, manufactured now by all, in each direction.

"Merz. Skidded," she told him. She thought she thought a glimpse of the blonde girl, almost directly ahead of her, but could not keep sight long enough to tell.

"I'm sorry," he was saying, animated now for the first time since he'd arrived. The loudspeakers began to sputter. The noise of spectators dropped away at once.

"Otto Merz is dead. Otto Merz is dead. Otto Merz is dead."

Thea had been introduced to Merz by Walter at last night's hideous party. They had exchanged names. Today at the photo session he had nodded briefly in her direction; and she had dipped her head in return.

Sam inhaled. The collar of his shirt was wet where he'd splashed water to revive himself.

The noise of spectators was continuous now. Every few moments it would subdue, as if in anticipation of further announcement, then return to the previous level. There was something in it of the pulsing of airplane engines the day before. Merz had been a large man, and had moved without any particular grace.

The woman behind her screamed again and again.

"I'm sorry," Sam was repeating.

She listened to the rain, heavier now, beating against the green canvas canopy. Later today, the Chancellor was due to address all Germany by radio, from a rally in

Königsberg, at a Day of National Awakening; and Thea wondered if he would speak of Merz, and of his tragic fate.

Then Thea was on her toes, scanning the horizon. Off to the right, just above the tree line, she thought she could make out a puff of black, thickened smoke.

The last time Thea had been on a film set was the chemical factory explosion, in *Testament*. It was the final night of shooting. She had been standing next to Lang and cameraman Fritz Arno Wagner on the ten-meter-high platform. Beside her was a small, harmless-looking model of the chemical factory, with a number of colored buttons. From the buttons mysterious wires went out to the real factory, which lay spread out before them in the glare of innumerable spotlights. Then Lang started blowing up the factory, simply by pressing the buttons. She recalled now the first of the four gigantic chimneys, seventy meters high, falling sideways amid thunderous noise and enormous clouds of dust.

Thea found herself moved beyond expectation by the death of Mercedes driver Merz.

She heard herself say, "It is a sad day for Germany," and was immediately sorry; because it was something Sam would not understand, and the remark would only create friction between them. Then the small blonde child, four rows ahead, was pointing in her direction.

Thea was an admirer of the Bauhaus, and was pleased to see that the new concrete building on the edge of the UFA lot awaited only the most final touches. The light bulbs, bare the week before, were now ensconced in hubs of ground glass. It was Monday morning, the sixth of March. Saturday night, in dense fog, they had been the last plane allowed to land at Tempelhof. (She heard later that the Chancellor himself had had trouble getting back from Königsberg, and found herself obscurely pleased.) She'd left Sam at the airport and gone straight to Breitenbachplatz, to find Lang behind the door of his study. There were feverish typing sounds from within, and she assumed he was working furiously on his solo inspiration. On Sunday a stubbled Lang emerged for lunch, but retreated to his study when Thea suggested a stroll. In the evening she insisted he eat something; and he'd joined her, for liver pâté and cheeses. He was too preoccupied, far too "elsewhere," to be foul.

"This new script," he'd said, bringing a seeded roll to his face with so little attention Thea was not sure he'd hit his mouth. "It's much more Viennese than anything we've done recently."

"More of your childhood?"

Lang said, "Exactly," in a tone which gave no sign he'd heard her question, the inflection she'd put on it. Half of the roll was in his mouth. "Why don't you drop by the lot tomorrow," he said finally, "for lunch in the commissary?"

There was certainly no use in talking to him now. "Perfect," she told Lang.

"If I'm not with Correll," he said, already on his way back to the study, roll in one hand, a glass of milk in the other, "I'll be in the screening room." He'd taken a sip of the milk, leaving a narrow white mustache, turned, and was gone.

Now, hand on the knob of the screening room door, Thea readied a quick entrance. She opened the door a discreet quarter swing, but there was no darkness, nothing being projected; and the room was, if anything, brighter than the corridor. Lang and a younger man with dark curly hair were seated on the apron of the flooring between the front row of seats and the screen. The man sat cross-legged; Lang was kneeling, as if shooting craps.

"—eyeshades, so he could sleep on the set," the curly-headed man went on. It was Edgar Ulmer, who had worked with Murnau, and had been production designer for *Nibelungen*, *Metropolis*, and *Spies*. Thea had not seen him in a year or two, and tried to recall now what she'd heard he'd been up to.

"Iron Stoves," said Lang. Then, at her approach, "Darling."

"Thea," said Ulmer.

"Edgar. Fritz." She took a seat in the front row, but felt uncomfortable seated before two men whose eyes were at the level of her knees.

"Fortunate man," said Ulmer. "Do you think he knows that he is married to the best scenario writer in Germany?"

Thea rose, walked over to the men, sat abruptly, joining them on the apron. "He knows sometimes."

Lang ran a knuckle down the edge of her neck.

"We were talking about Dieterle," Ulmer said. His eyebrows grew together, and Thea could see the stubble, at the bridge of his nose, where he shaved them, so they did not seem to join. "He wore white gloves and his wife was all day onstage with him saying, 'William, it's enough. Now you must rest.' "

"Handing him the eyeshade," added Lang. She noticed her husband had taken some care with his dress today. There was a handkerchief in his breast pocket.

"I'm glad you're back," she told Ulmer. She remembered now that Ulmer had gone to the United States after
Spies; and seemed to recall being told, by the cinematographer Schufftan, that he lived there now.

"I go back tomorrow," Ulmer said.

Lang said, "Hollywood."

"Dieterle and Murnau were both actors at Reinhardt's
when I was there," Ulmer went on, letting cigarette ash
drop to the new carpeting. "Dieterle we called Iron Stoves
because he was a tall guy, not talented, but whenever we
needed somebody in armor he had to play those parts, so
we called him Iron Stoves. We were very vicious kids."
She watched him look around for an ashtray. He could
not have been more than thirty-five.

"Hollywood," Lang repeated. The room went dark. A
second later three pale rectangles of light, from the booth,
appeared high up on the far wall. Then all went black.
Now the rectangles reappeared, much brighter.

"Hello?" The voice came from the booth, as lights
went back on.

"Down here," said Lang, blinking a bit, and fussing
with the monocle.

The lights in the booth went out. Soon the door
opened, and Nebenzal entered.

"I couldn't find the right switch," Nebenzal said.

"Seymour," said Ulmer.

"Edgar. Fritz. Thea." He occupied the chair in the
front row which she had vacated. He was holding a sheet
of pink paper, with raggedly chamfered corners. "What are
you all doing here?" Nebenzal said finally.

"Hiding from you," said Lang, deadpan. It occurred

to Thea that she was the only woman in the room, and quite probably the only person not a Jew.

"You have an assignment for me?" said Ulmer. "How sweet." Thea could see black marks, on the blank side of the paper, as if it had been the product of the early, overinked part of a mimeograph run.

Lang put an arm to Ulmer's shoulder. "Everyone's a director these days," Lang said.

"Bad news," said Nebenzal.

The sheet in his hand was shaking as he held it out to Lang.

Lang looked at Nebenzal and took hold of the thing.

Ulmer had been readying a terrible face, with wrinkled nose and puffed cheeks, in retaliation for Lang's remark. Now he recomposed his features.

Lang scanned the paper, and held it out for Thea to see. It was the mimeo'd schedule for UFA-Palast. Three corners had bites taken out of them, one a small hole. The thing must have been affixed, Thea thought, by thumbtacks, only one of which Nebenzal had taken the care to remove, before ripping it down.

"Shit," Lang said.

"It went up today," Nebenzal was saying.

Thea looked at the pink paper, until it hit her that *The Testament of Doctor Mabuse* had been scheduled to premiere at UFA-Palast on the twenty-third. Opposite March 23 on this schedule was *Wounded Germany*.

Lang looked at Ulmer. *"Testament,"* he told him, "has seemingly been rescheduled."

"A silly mistake," said Ulmer, making no effort to put conviction into it.

Lang was on his feet, and had one arm inside his leather overcoat, which had been lying folded neatly across two seats.

"Kallmann is off skiing, in Switzerland. Correll is right here, but doesn't return my calls," said Nebenzal.

Lang said, "Shitheads."

He hit the door of the screening room. Nebenzal was behind him, then Thea and Ulmer. Outside Lang took long steps but did not break into a run. The sky was uniformly blue, with tender streaks of cumulonimbus, and seemed lower, flatter than usual. Thea caught up to her husband, who put an arm around her and slowed, so she could keep up, in her dress shoes. There was a curving pebbled path between the new building and the old, but Lang took a more direct route over iced lawn.

"Pigs," said Lang. It was several degrees above freezing; but Lang's exclamation produced a small, emphatic cloud in front of his mouth.

Thea could hear Ulmer, some steps behind, explaining to Nebenzal that he was "with them on this one."

"It may be nothing," Nebenzal said.

Ulmer said, "Not a chance."

Thea put a hand to her husband's neck, squeezed in reassurance. Breathless now, she disengaged from him, to walk more slowly. Ulmer caught up with her. He was smiling. "We assault the Black Tower?" he said. It was the familiar name for UFA's old administration building, three-story, mock Gothic.

Inside Lang spun right, the others trailing him down the waxed corridor whose high ceilings and hard, echoic surfaces seemed, like many of Ulmer's sets, intentionally to dwarf human aspiration. Lang paused at the corner for his entourage to catch up, then turned left toward the commissary. Two men, executives of some sort, nodded professionally at the quartet without interrupting their conversation. They were followed by a man with an eyepatch, in pirate regalia. As they passed the stairwell Thea tried to recall what they were shooting on the large stage now. Another suited man tried to catch Lang's regard, but was not successful.

The UFA commissary—a large square room with tables for four and six, banquettes around the sides—hid behind two oversized arched oak doors. The old uniformed man whose name, Thea remembered, was Karl, made for the vertical brass handle, but was beaten to it by Lang, who put a good deal of effort into opening the door, at a rate faster than its pneumatic hinge would seem to allow. It was lunchtime. Lang made directly for the near corner, whose slightly raised round table was visible from all parts of the room, and at which one did not sit without invitation.

"Herr Correll," said Lang to the seated man, UFA's head of production, who had been sipping from a glass of iced water.

Correll smiled. Rudolf Klein-Rogge, beside him, patted the hair at his temple and gazed shyly at his ex-wife.

"What kind of shit is this?" said Lang, presenting the pink schedule. It was warm in the commissary, and Lang's monocle, chilled from the walk, had misted over. The maître d' was striding toward them, several huge menus in hand, but stopped, some distance away, at the sight of Correll's raised fingertips.

"Thea," said Klein-Rogge.

"I've been trying to reach you all morning," said Correll, letting the paper fall to the table, in the manner of one declining service of a warrant. Klein-Rogge adjusted his plate to cover the accumulation of crumbs and poppyseeds he'd produced while breaking and buttering a hard roll.

"Thea, you are looking well," Correll went on. She watched him scan the room, moving the tips of his fingers in sequence, as if performing arithmetic. "You must join us," he said finally.

Lang slid toward him, at the banquette. Ulmer took the space to Klein-Rogge's right, which the actor had been patting. Waiters appeared, holding chairs for Thea, and for Nebenzal.

"Vichyssoise for all," said Correll.

Lang lifted a hard pat of butter with the tip of his knife.

"*Nibelungen*," said Correll. "Edgar should really tell this one. Two years' work. Fritz carried it to the Palast reel by reel, because he was still cutting. Before your time, Seymour. While the second reel was running, this man cut the third. Meanwhile Kellogg had been negotiating all day, and that night the gold mark was born. Seven hundred thousand marks were now one gold mark, and the picture cost us not a penny!"

Ulmer said, "*Testament.*"

"A picture, Edgar, UFA can be proud of," said Correll, wiping the sweat from the outside of his water glass. "A picture which would, moreover, prove its worthiness at the box office."

Two waiters busied themselves setting down bowls of soup.

"And we know that the audience wants another *Mabuse*," Correll said.

Klein-Rogge nodded.

"Then what happened?" said Lang quietly.

"Arguably Rudolf's best work." Correll patted the actor's wrist.

Ulmer began work on the soup. Lang's monocle was clear now, catching light from the floor-to-ceiling windows at the near wall. The windows were covered with new gauzy drapes which sighed and fluttered in the faint breeze. Lang had not let go, Thea saw, of the butter knife. It was midday; and the indirect light, filtered through provocative off-white curtains, lent to all the appearance of their best complexion.

"I fought all morning," Correll said finally.

"You're a dead man," said Lang.

Nebenzal said, "Fritz."

"You're a dead man," Lang repeated.

Thea looked at Klein-Rogge, who returned the regard. The men at the table were discussing a film she had written, and whether it would be shown, as if it had nothing to do with her.

"Just tell us what happened." Nebenzal put thumb and forefinger to his upper lip, as if to ensure that his mustache would not fall off.

The maître d' reappeared, holding a palm-sized notepad. Lang, Thea, and Nebenzal ordered veal, Klein-Rogge a salad, Correll the fish of the day, Ulmer sausage. The maître d' went away and his assistants arrived, filling water glasses with a show of unobtrusiveness. Correll said, "I really don't know anything, firsthand."

The room's light decreased slightly, which Thea attributed to a cloud, passing the unseen sun. When the curtains blew toward the windows she could see the lattice shadow-grid of leading between panes, which was lost to diffusion when they blew roomward once more. She wondered when UFA had decided it was spring, and replaced the heavy damask draperies that had adorned the commissary since November.

"What *do* you know?" asked Nebenzal, as if talking to a child, not yet of the age of reason, who has misplaced something of great value.

Correll said: "Dr. Goebbels called Hugenberg. Goebbels said he would have to ban the film, because it showed that a determined group of men could succeed in overturning any government by brute force."

Flatware clinked sharp and reverberant against china. The room tone seemed to alter, recede, the way a train's noise shifts as it emerges from a tunnel. It was time, Thea knew, to think seriously about what she'd been referring to in mental shorthand as "the Eastern project." Arabic, not Oriental, she was sure of it now. Thea put fingers to her ears, pressing the flaps, listening to the overlapping roar of conversation. She could make it woosh away, and reassert itself, in satisfying, modulated waves.

"He said the presentation of criminal acts committed against human society was so detailed and fascinating it might lead to similar attacks against lives and property, and to terrorist actions against the state."

"Where's Hugenberg?" Lang said.

Thea recalled an idea she had once jotted down, about hashish smugglers, and saw briefly, in mind's eye, the face of the blonde child, from Nürburgring; and thought about the ways that plot, that image, might begin to play off one another.

Correll said, "Calling on Papen. He got eight percent at the polls yesterday. It's not the best of days to be bothering him."

"Are you telling me," Lang asked, "he's not available?"

"Yes."

Hugenberg, according to this morning's *Vöss*, which she'd read over breakfast, had done quite badly; and the Nazis, though strong, had failed to get a majority. She supposed they were in for another month of "visiting." A German child, kidnaped by Arab *hashishins*.

Lang said, "Oh." Then he said, "I'm sorry," and rose from the table.

The butter knife lay absently in his hand, and he took it with him as he turned away. The faint breeze sucked the gauze curtains against the windows, imprinting them with dark, regular crossbars.

"I *am* Mabuse," said Klein-Rogge to no one in particular. He tried out a smile, then removed it.

Lang was out the door.

"Things will settle down in a couple of days," said Correll when no one else spoke. "Perhaps, Seymour, we can get by with editing. Some cuts. Some new dialogue." Chemical factory in flames, one chimney after another collapsing as the hapless inspector looks on, once again too late. Smoke hisses from the engine carrying chemicals away from the danger zone. Fire engines, bells clanging furiously, converge upon the factory: water from their hoses plays upon the collapsing building, mingling with flame and smoke. Police sirens, enormous headlights raking the bushes, motorcycles rev up, the hooting of cars, toward the grand finale, of light, sound, fire. In the chase which follows, bushes seem to give way in bundles; and the leaves, above the heads of the pursuers, dissolve into blobs of motion. Ghostly white milestones, by the side of the road, eerily illuminated by the fleeting headlights of the criminal auto. The last will of Doctor Mabuse.

"You should have told us," Nebenzal was saying to Correll. "You really should have told us."

Then Lang was once more at the table, reseating himself on the cool leather banquette. Ulmer was just finishing his sausages.

Lang said, "I'd just started writing something, and now my concentration is broken." He turned toward Correll and said, "You cost me work."

Thea looked across at Klein-Rogge, her ex-husband, who had been an actor for years and years, and who could understand her at times like this.

F I V E

THEY STOPPED HIM ON THE GRAVEL PATH
which led from the new UFA building. "Herr Lang," said
the taller of the two, without the inflection usually lent to
a question. He wore his hat low, shadowing a whitish scar
which ran from the corner of his eye to the edge of his
mouth. The other was more squat, with large hands of no
distinction.

"Yes?" Lang could not quite recall where he knew
them from. The one without the scar resembled, but was
not, his chief electrician from *Metropolis*.

"You know this man?" asked the tall one, looking
downward. Lang followed his eyes. He seemed to be holding something in half-curved fingers, an inept conjuror
palming a card.

"Take your time," said the squat companion.

The one with the scar brought his cupped hand to chest
level. It held the photograph of a man. It was clear, from
the way he held it, that Lang was to look but not to touch.

"You know this man," he repeated. It was, this time,
somewhat more declarative. His companion was holding
an aluminum film canister. Lang had seen them before: in
Humm's office, just after he'd had the cavity filled.

The squat man was chewing gum, or tobacco. The
two were walking now down the gravel path toward the

111

stages. Lang walked with them. He'd not been walking in that direction previously.

"No," said Lang, glancing at the photograph, which was of a man with curly brown hair in his early thirties, wearing a cloth cap at jaunty angle. Lang stopped, inserted his monocle, caught up. He regarded the photo more intently.

"No," Lang said finally. They had turned right, and were walking toward the new building now.

"We have some film," said the one with the canister.

"—which you should watch," the other completed.

The squat man with the canister offered Lang an American cigarette, an Old Gold. Lang declined, extracting a Boyard. He probed his breast pocket for matches, found instead a rectangular envelope containing a pair of theater tickets. They were for Kaiser and Weill's *The Silver Lake*, directed by Detlef Sierck, a handsome young man Lang knew from UFA parties, years back.

The squat man was holding out a small, exquisitely detailed lighter.

"Wieland," said the other.

It was not clear whether the tall man with the scar was giving his own name, introducing his companion, or giving identity to the man in the photo. Lang watched him replace the photo in his shirt pocket, extend his right hand. "Wieland," he repeated. Lang shook the proffered hand, and said, "Pleased."

Silver Lake's premiere, in Leipzig three weeks ago, had been disrupted by SA brownshirts, who'd shouted the actors down. Lang's tickets were to the play's Berlin opening, which was to have taken place the following week but which instead had been "indefinitely postponed."

"Bott," the squat one was saying, gazing seriously at the tip of his Old Gold.

It was Wednesday. The sky was a dark blue, the air transparent. Lang found his eye attracted to detail work at the tops of buildings. Then they were at the door to the new structure. He'd meant to take Thea to *Silver Lake*. That night, having been informed of the "postponement" by phone, they ate listless omelets, staring at the fireplace fire until ten, when Thea went out for a walk. She paused only to take a flower from the vase in her bedroom and place it in the cut-glass vase on the hall table. Lang had counted to forty, then dialed Lily; but she'd not been at home, and was not home by midnight, which was the latest he felt comfortable calling. An editorial in the *Beobachter*, which Nebenzal had shown him, said that "Sierck, who took on the production for the Leipzig Altes Theater and directed it, has rendered a service to the Berlin literary intelligentsia and its outdated intellectual satellites, which stands to cost him very dear indeed."

Now it was the third day in a row of clear skies and warm weather. Lang was finding his topcoat nearly superfluous. They were at the door to the new concrete building.

Bott went in first, followed by Lang, then Wieland. Bott handed the canister to Pfeiffer who took it and made for the booth, as if by prearrangement. Pfeiffer did not meet Lang's eye. Then Wieland was ushering them into the screening room. Lang took the chair just left of center, fifth row, as was his custom. The two sat just over Lang's right shoulder. He realized that Bott, who had offered the Old Gold, was the good cop, Wieland the bad. It was a division of labor Thea had written into their scenarios, and which he'd always assumed a reflection of actual methodology. Then the film began, and sputtered a bit, before Pfeiffer hit the lights, and pulled the thing into focus.

The first shot was of the Tiergarten, midwinter. It was quite grained, and choppy, as if shot hand-held. Lang watched a man in cap and tweed overcoat walk toward the camera, which spun away abruptly. Black leader. The camera, in a car now, sweeping a broad commercial street, perhaps Friedrichstrasse. The camera picked up and held the same man, now hatless. The man in the film, like the one in the photo they'd shown him, had curly hair; but Lang could not be sure, one way or the other, whether they were the same.

Black leader, flecked with white, for about fifteen seconds. Then the same shot, repeated.

"His name is Sam Harrison," said Wieland, studying Lang's face in the flickering cinema light.

Harrison, in the tweed coat, entering a door. Another shot, same angle, taken with a wider lens, identifying the legend above that door, HOTEL VOM EPOCH.

More black leader.

The door of the hotel. A woman enters. Her carriage is unmistakable, as is the way she clutches her handbag.

"Born Philadelphia eight January 1901," Wieland was saying. "U.S. passport, occupation listed 'writer.' Fluent in French, English, German."

A high-angle shot of a crowd gathered in demonstration. The footage once more seems hand-held, as if the camera were lifted above someone's head, as he worked through the crowd. A two-second slice of this footage, reprinted several times and spliced end to end, of the camera panning three faces. The one in the middle has curly hair. Lang can just make out the stubble along the man's jawline, which gives way to the coarse grain of high-speed film stock.

Once again, the entrance of the Hotel vom Epoch.

"Have you seen enough?" asked Bott quietly. Lang nodded. Bott stood up and ran most of the way down the aisle, waving at the booth with two arms as if flagging down a train. The lights went on, and the film was stopped. Bott slid into the seat next to Lang's. He took an Old Gold and offered one to Lang, which Lang this time around did not decline. Wieland sat on Lang's other side.

"I've never met him," Lang told Wieland, who was removing a black Morocco-bound notebook from his breast pocket.

"Detained and questioned by Paris police following a disturbance in the Café Maldoror, February of 1930." Wieland read from the notebook, held at an angle away from Lang. "A disturbance in which several members of the Surrealist group were arrested or detained."

"I've never met him," Lang found himself repeating, quite softly now. He listened to the faint, reassuring clatter, from the projection booth, of film being rewound.

"In 1931, according to information compiled by French sources, subject—"

Lang stood up and said, "I don't want to hear this." Bott put his arm along Lang's shoulder, in the gesture of fraternal solace. Lang worked crabwise down the aisle toward the exit. In the corridor Lang noticed the new carpeting. He wondered whether they would leave the concrete walls bare, or cover them with something hideous. Thea's American was far younger than he, and handsome in a way he had never been. The carpet was put down badly with gaps at the seams. Lang knew that it would buckle, before very long.

"Come," said Wieland, notebook protruding now from the handkerchief pocket of his double-breasted overcoat. Bott was waiting by the door of the booth. Wieland ushered Lang outdoors. Lang held his forearm to his head, shielding his eyes from the glare to which he was now unaccustomed. Lang wondered briefly whether he should ask Wieland for some form of identification; but it seemed too late for that now and there was no way to do it, really, without sounding silly.

"Bott said I was cruel to do this to you, Herr Lang. Perhaps he was right." They were in step now, crunching gravel synchronously. He had done no work on his new scenario, *The Legend of the Last Viennese Fiaker*, since late Sunday night; and given all, he could see how it might take some time before he regained that composure which would enable him to sit down and write once more.

Wieland was saying: "But I felt you should know the truth."

In the few days since he'd stopped writing, the story had been coming together for him; and now he visualized it fluently, all of a piece.

"Your films teach us, Herr Lang, that it is best to know the truth."

The Fiaker is the owner and driver of a beautifully maintained carriage. With a haughty graciousness he gives the man who tends his horses—the lowly Waterer—a lottery ticket he has been forced to buy, but which he believes beneath his dignity to keep. The Waterer, of course, wins a fortune, which he invests in an automobile factory. Social barriers between the Fiaker and the Waterer break down in the solvent of the latter's new wealth; and the Waterer's son is at last able to marry his beloved, the Fiaker's daughter.

Gravel had given way to cobbles, and they were now on the UFA backlot, in the simulated city used for urban exteriors. Two streets of three-story tenements met in a shallow V. Occasionally, Lang caught a glimpse through a window of the wooden armature and scaffolding which was all that lay behind. He'd used this set in *M*. There were six streetlamps, which he'd had fitted with "ring-of-fire" du-Arcs. Lang had them wet the cobbles, for increased reflectivity, and light a few of the windows from behind. Then waited, for nightfall.

"In Trier, last Friday," Wieland went on, sitting on the second step of a stoop, somewhat gingerly, lest it not hold his weight, "Harrison wandered around on his own for several hours. I overheard him enquiring where he might find the birthplace of Karl Marx." Lang found himself on the stoop, one tread down from Wieland, whom he could not see without turning his head. Metal rails, laid down for a camera dolly on the far side of the cobbles, caught a bit of the sun, bounced it painfully back at him. The stoop was the color and texture of worn stone but was not as cool to the touch as real stone would have been.

"He sent two wires to France, on the plans of Mercedes to reenter racing, plans which have only been announced officially this morning."

The Fiaker retains but one consolation: the damned horseless carriages are not allowed on the principal allée of the Prater. Then, as the two fathers-in-law toast the couple with new wine, a headline flies across the screen. EXTRA:

AUTOMOBILES NOW PERMITTED ON THE ALLÉE. All illusions shattered, the Fiaker suffers a fatal stroke.

"—and though we have no firm reports from our counterparts in Spain, it is perhaps more than coincidental that we note Harrison's presence in Barcelona, and in Casas Viejas, this January. At the very moment of the anarcho-syndicalist upsurge."

Lang had moved to his right, to escape the reflected glare, but now found himself having to move once more. He listened to the sound of Wieland's notebook flipping shut. Then Wieland was beside him. Lang recalled the slow tracking shot of Peter Lorre, psychopathic child molester, sauntering down this very street, whistling an air from Grieg, his signature. Then Lorre paused at the far stoop, and Lang moved the camera all the way in. He liked to track slowly, inexorably from wide-shot right into the face. Eyes, lips, pores, at the very moment when the man realized just how far things have gone: and just how sinkingly futile all his plans to escape destiny.

"If you want, Herr Lang, we can have him picked up."

The rest of the *Fiaker* story, Lang knew, would take place in Heaven, a Viennese filigree Heaven, all white lace and decorative pastry. As far as he'd gotten, Saint Peter lets the Fiaker in, but refuses permission for the horses and coach. There was a happy ending, Lang knew, just within reach. Now Lang felt a coolness at his forehead. He brought his hand up, and it came down wet. He did not like it, that Wieland was watching him sweat; and wondered when Bott, the good cop, was scheduled to return.

"Have you spoken with my wife?" Lang asked finally.

Wieland looked drawn, tired. "We thought it best to leave that to the discretion of the husband."

Lang said, "Yes."

"Shall we leave it to you then?" Wieland did not look as if he were enjoying his work. Lang watched him shelter his eyes from the dolly-rail reflection.

Lang rose and nodded.

"I told him," said Wieland, "that in all likelihood you had never met him. It was insisted that I ask." Lang felt within himself the power to have Thea's American taken from her. The power, short of that, to fill her life with a miserable knowledge. He could only think that he wanted to wait until he felt surer of himself before deciding. He felt a cooling breeze against his face.

"They are setting us up," Lang said to Wieland as they walked, on gravel now once more. "A week or two more of skies like this. Then blizzards."

Wieland said, "It has been remarkable though. Since the election. They are calling it 'Hitler weather.' " Wieland pinched the bridge of his nose. "If I may," he went on, "without embarrassing either of us unduly: let me tell you how much I enjoy *Metropolis*. I have seen it countless times."

"My least favorite film," Lang heard himself say, in unaccustomed candor.

Wieland's eyes drifted leftward in recollection. Then, addressing Lang, he said, "The empty stairwell. The empty attic. An unused plate on the kitchen table. A remote patch of grass with Elsie's ball lying upon it. And a balloon, catching in telegraph wires."

It hit him that Wieland was reciting, shot by shot, the sequence from *M*, as Elsie's mother calls out, in final desperation, the name of her child. Lang could only assume that Wieland had seen it numerous times, or that

119

the powers of observation, developed in police work, served him well at the movies. "The very balloon," Lang replied idly, "which the murderer had bought from the blind beggar, to win Elsie's confidence." They were quite near the old building, where Lang had been before Bott and Wieland had intercepted him. A squat man, whom Lang took at this distance to be Bott, stood just to the side of the building's steps.

"Fräulein von Harbou's scenario," he told Wieland.

Lang was on Wieland's left, and could see the thin, whitish scar. "The police in your films," Wieland was saying, "always win. And yet they are never as compelling as those they pursue."

"I don't know what to say to that." Lang smiled.

Bott came up, holding the canister.

"It's been an honor to meet you," said Wieland.

Lang took the proffered hand absently. He found himself thinking of *Testament* which, he felt sure now, would never see release. Hugenberg was in negotiation with Hitler: the latter had gotten forty-four percent of the vote in Sunday's election, and needed the support of Hugenberg's pathetic Nationalists to form a government. "Surely Hugenberg can demand the release of *Testament*," Ulmer had suggested, after their extravagantly upsetting lunch, "as a condition for support, yes? Isn't that how things are done? Don't look at me, my friend. I'm on the first train tomorrow." Lang had laughed. Now he wondered whether his wife's association with an undesirable had had anything to do with Goebbels's decision. He doubted it. Pfeiffer had told him: Goebbels didn't like the ending. What more reason did they need, to ban a film? Of course, if it ever turned out that Thea's affair had been in any sense a factor, Lang would have one more matter to add to the list of those things which he could never forgive. It was something Ulmer would understand; but Ulmer had left for Paris yesterday, taking with him Robert and Curt Siodmak. The Siodmaks, of a Leipzig banking family, were Jewish, and felt compelled, Ulmer had told him, to leave.

"Please let us know," Wieland was saying, holding out an outsized business card of the old style, "if we can be of any assistance to you, in this, or any other matter." There was no way, Lang thought, that Hugenberg, Goebbels, any of them, could object to the *The Legend of the Last Viennese Fiaker*. He would sit down tonight and see if he could finish it, writing without distraction, unconcerned by those events which, he decided, he would enter in his diary under the heading of "Hotel vom Epoch."

Wieland went on, "I'm pleased that we could get this cleared up." Lang had seen *Wounded Germany*, the film which would replace *Testament* at UFA-Palast. It was an embarrassment, a joke. It was put together by Johannes Haussler, who directed with his asshole. Did anyone really need to see the funeral of Horst Wessel?

"Herr Lang?" Bott, film canister wedged beneath his armpit, held out the pack of Old Golds.

Lang made to wave the offer away, but his gesture was ill timed, and excessively forceful. Lang felt his hand slap against that of the policeman. The canister hit the gravel with great clatter and opened. The pack of cigarettes landed a meter or so to Lang's right. He listened to the lid of the film can make wonking noises, increasingly rapid, and of successively higher pitch, as it settled.

121

"I'm sorry," he told Bott. Lang bent over to pick up the Old Golds but found them farther away than he had judged. He had to take several steps in a crouch before reaching them.

"My fault," said Bott, who was, he recalled now, the good cop. Bott replaced the lid of the canister. The reel had been full almost to the rim, leading Lang to think he'd been shown only small fraction of the footage.

Lang handed Bott the pack. Bott mechanically offered it to Lang who took a crumpled cigarette, and waited for Bott's lighter. Lang had been shown, in grainy black and white, the face of his rival; and had not been laid waste. Still he found himself possessed by a loss, profound and obscure, a child's balloon tangled among telegraph wires, converging toward the horizon.

"It's nothing," said Bott, holding the exquisite lighter in his slabby hand. Wieland was looking at him, or perhaps at the approach of Bott's flame, reflected in the monocle.

"Do you want to keep this?" Wieland asked, extending the photograph of Sam Harrison with two fingers. Lang took a last look. The curly-haired man was standing in front of a brick wall, face front, as if awaiting a firing squad. There was something about the staggered layering of the bricks which was familiar to Lang. He was sure, at once, that the man was standing in front of Miës van der Rohe's monument to Karl Liebknecht and Rosa Luxemburg. He could see the point of the metal star in the upper right corner of the photo. Lang considered telling them where the picture had been taken, but on reflection thought it best not to.

Wieland smiled, and said, "We have copies."

"No," Lang said, waving it away.

In November of 1918, when Lang was twenty-seven, news reached Vienna of the uprising at Kiel, and of the revolution in Germany which was spreading, it seemed, by the hour. There were eight men in Lang's hospital ward, and they took shifts at the radio, waking the others when necessary. (Lang was on day leave, and had to report back to the hospital at seven each evening. But when morning came he did not leave for home, or a café, as was his custom. He stayed on the ward, listening to the radio.) Then there was no way they could stand the confinement of the hospital.

Lang and five of the others—all those who could, stretching the term, be considered "ambulatory"—went down two flights to street level. There was no one at the desk to stop them. The manifestation had begun that morning, with a rally in solidarity with the mutiny and revolution in Germany. Now it was late afternoon, and the demonstration continued, as if it were demanding much else, perhaps all else. Lang found himself in the streets, embarrassed by his hospital whites, which he'd neglected to change. But it did not really seem to matter. A man next to him, balding, unshaven, in pajamas, heaved a cobblestone through the window of Zilboorg's variety store. Scanning the plaza, Lang realized he had lost sight of his ward mates, but this too seemed not to matter.

"*Join us*," Lang heard himself say. It was such a cliché, something to say at a political manifestation. He said it again, then once more. Lang watched two policemen, on horseback, charging the edge of the crowd. Their horses toppled, and a great cheer went up. "*Join us*," he repeated, with somewhat less irony, and again, until the italics dropped away, and he was yelling, and the cobble in his hand went toward the shattered Zilboorg's window. It fell short. He was worried lest his hospital slippers not protect him from the shards and rubble in the street.

Someone said, "Cologne has fallen!" It occurred to Lang that he had not used his right arm for anything but eating since he'd been wounded; and that the cobble had gone pretty far, considering. They were in a side street now, quite narrow, six-story buildings on each side. It would get direct sunlight only at the noon hour. It was nearly dusk.

Now, standing in front of the UFA administration building with Wieland and Bott, Lang knew that the manifestation ended the next morning, and that he reentered the hospital freely, to wait out the Armistice. But in the alley, he had not known it was going to end. Had no way of telling this was not the way it would always be. In the alley, listening to police horses on the avenue, he felt smarter than he had in his life, and knew at once that most of the things he thought of as natural, or destined, were in fact quite arbitrary. He wanted more than he had ever known before. The paving stones were damp, and cool to the touch.

Back in the hospital, waiting for the end of hostilities, he remembered some of what had come to him in the alleyway, enough to know that he could not go back to architecture. To do that would be to enclose his life at sea, and in the war, within parentheses, as an episode. Perhaps four times a year since then Lang recalled his day and night in the streets in a way which was not anecdotal. Looking now from Wieland to Bott, and back again, he wondered why he had ever thought it enough, just to make film.

"Keep the pack," Bott was saying. Lang went for it, found himself still holding Wieland's business card, somewhat curved now from the way he'd been cupping it. He slipped the card and the Old Golds into his inside breast pocket, feeling once more the *Silver Lake* tickets, useless now.

"Thank you," he told Bott; and it occurred to him that it would probably be best to speak with Nebenzal, right away, to tell Nebenzal to get hold of the negative of *Testament*, and put it somewhere safe.

Lang knew, now, the ending for *Fiaker*. Saint Peter rushes off to arrange a special concert for Saint Cecile. Although all the great composers have been invited, he can't seem to find them. He discovers them on comfortable clouds listening in bliss to the Fiaker singing Viennese lieder.

He reports the matter to Our Lord, who arrives at the gates to speak with the coachman. The Fiaker refuses to budge without his horses. The Lord appoints him His special coachman, gets into the carriage; and the proud Fiaker drives Him into Heaven. As the wheels turn a new constellation is born: The Big Wagon.

"Good-bye," Wieland was saying.

"Good-bye." Lang knew his ending now. He could not wait to get home and write it.

The waiter paused, then set down her third demitasse. Thea fitted a cigarette into the ebony holder which she rested on the tabletop while stirring coffee. The tiny spoon made spiral galaxies of light-brown foam. She removed the spoon, looked up at the modern clock overhead. It was four, and he was now an hour late. She'd give him another fifteen minutes, no more. She broke a sugar cube, peeled the paper from one half, dropped it into the cup. Small bubbles rose to the surface, where they joined others at the jagged shores along the rim, or in the central cluster with its drawn-out spirals. It was still swirling somewhat. He'd said, on the phone, that he'd meet her "at the café," and she'd assumed Sam meant the Romanische, as was their custom. The cigarette had soaked up water from the tabletop, and she replaced it with a fresh one. As she brought the flame closer, it occurred to her that perhaps he'd been referring to the Café Zuntz, down the street. He'd often complained of the "shitheads from Ku-damm" who were making the Romanische uninhabitable. The Zuntz, where they'd met once or twice, was smaller, and had yet to be written up by the weeklies. Still it was quite unlikely he'd intended them to rendezvous at the Zuntz without having specified the smaller café by name. Thea blew across the top of the cup, took a sip. She unwrapped, and stirred in, the other half cube. She'd not brought anything to read. There was a notepad in her pocketbook, but she'd always felt silly, writing in a café. She would not wait past the end of this cigarette, or four-fifteen, whichever came later. She would try the Zuntz; then go home. Thea looked from the big clock to her demitasse. The bubble-raft galaxies within revolved in a direction opposite to that of the Romanische clock's second hand, and at something like the same speed.

Departing the café, she gave a glance to the Romanische's

other room, the "swimming pool," where the artists hung out, on the off chance that Sam would be among them; but he was not. Outside, she faced the Kaiser Wilhelm Gedächtniskirche, her view of its steps obscured, save intermittent flashes afforded by the occasional gap in a steady stream of cyclists. Perhaps they were returning home from work. She found herself momentarily lost, cyclists, motorists reduced to patterns of light and dark, streaming horizontally, sound bearing no correspondence to the machines which produced it. Then at once Thea knew where she was, and turned right down Tauentzienstrasse toward the Zuntz. She had not eaten anything for hours save three cups of coffee. To her left, walking into traffic, was a young man with a wide-brimmed hat and gaucho vest.

Then she saw Sam, on the other side of the street, hand-held movie camera pointed in her direction. She made to cross Tauentzienstrasse. A motorcycle passed between them. It was traveling at medium speed and carried in its tow a manacled man, appended by a length of thick chain. The cycle's driver wore a well-cut gray suit, with homburg. Thea looked to see Sam's camera panning with the bound man who, she could see now, was wrapped in a blanket, struggling to wriggle free. It was quite clear that if the man could not release himself from the chain he would be flayed and torn by the cobbles.

"Martini Szeny!" said the gaucho, in a tone quite reminiscent of Sam's carnival voice. Around the corner, protruding from a side street, Thea saw a wagon, of whose emblem she could see only

CIRCUS BU
Martini S

127

The motorcycle made a wide U-turn, scattering pedestrians. It came back toward her, then sped off toward the church; then left, onto Ku-Damm, without its freight. The bound man, not three meters in front of her, wriggled free of the remaining chains, flinging aside huge patches of shredded woolen blanket. He jumped up and down.

"Martini Szeny!" the gaucho declaimed. "The first star of the Mexican circus has once more unchained himself while dragged through the streets on a motorcycle!" Sam, who had spotted her, was waving now. Then the gray-suited cyclist came to a halt just beside her, front wheel in the air. He dismounted, bowing theatrically low, hat in front of him.

Sam crossed Tauentzienstrasse toward her, holding his camera aloft as if fording a stream with cargo he wished not to wet. He was sporting the cloth cap which she detested.

"My brother!" said Martini Szeny, a puddle of chains at his feet, one arm outflung toward the gray-suited man who had driven the cycle.

Sam pointed to the camera and grinned. "Money," he said.

"Circus Bustello, the true circus of Mexico!" The gaucho addressed the crowd, already dispersing.

"Let me buy you coffee," Sam was saying. She did not know just how to tell him that she'd been waiting an hour, and had run into him only by accident. Martini Szeny and the gaucho looked and sounded more like Gypsies than Mexicans. Thea tried to recall if she had seen Sam since Nürburgring, almost a week ago now. She decided she hadn't. It was Friday, and they'd been apart since Saturday night at Tempelhof. They were walking back toward the Romanische now.

"Had you been waiting long?" asked Sam as they reached the door.

Thea looked at him.

"I'm sorry," he said. Then, turning: "Let's go somewhere else."

Thea said, "Yes."

"Zuntz?"

"Fine." She was looking at his camera, which seemed new, and of a different shape than his Ciné-Kodak.

Inside, Sam ordered a double espresso, Thea a *vieux marc*. "They bought the Nürburgring footage," said Sam without preamble. "There's a great demand for actualities. Nadel says he'll pick up almost anything I can grab."

Thea released the butt of her previous cigarette from her Countess Told holder, inserted one of Sam's Camels. The habitués of the Zuntz seemed to be uniformly male, mid-thirties, with thick concave spectacles and stubble just shy of the length required for formal beard. Many were bent, in flagrantly bad posture, over foreign-language newspapers printed on the thin, crackly airmail stock whose rattle seemed the predominant room tone.

"With any luck," Sam was saying, "I can move out of the Epoch to what they call more suitable lodgings." Thea had never understood why he'd not moved out before, given the extent of the support he was receiving from Bala-Cynwyd. He lifted his cap, ran a hand through the dark curly hair which, it seemed to her, was perhaps more flecked with white than she'd recalled. It was an aging not reflected in his face, as unlined as ever. "There are friends in Paris I've not seen in ages," he was saying. "Perhaps you could join me."

"Depends," Thea said finally. She was one of two women in the room, the other a waitress. She wondered if this was where illustrators came when they needed life models for cartoon anarchists, the ones who always seem to be carrying spherical bombs, fuses flagrantly asputter.

Sam was wearing his gray shawl-collared sweater. "I think you would like Breton," he went on. Breton, the poet, was one of the names Sam would let fall when nostalgic for Paris. "And Thirion, Sadoul. Magritte, the man who painted my tie. Aragon. Jean Ferry." Some of the names were familiar. She could not discern whether Sam had spoken of them before, or whether she'd read about them in one of the monthlies. Probably both. The bohemians Thea knew in Berlin, as far as she could tell, expressed their disgust with society by eating soft-boiled eggs at four in the morning, or wearing dead flowers in their buttonholes. It was hard to tell just how well Sam knew this crew in Paris; and less clear that they were any more compelling than their Berlin counterparts.

"Let us leave for France tonight," Sam was saying.

"They're not going to release *The Testament of Doctor Mabuse*," said Thea quickly. It was, strangely, the first she'd told anyone. Sam was looking at her. "My film," she went on. "The one I was writing, when we met."

Sam toyed with the winding key of his new camera. "What happened?" he asked finally.

Thea said, "I don't know." She finished her brandy. "Politics."

"Not going to release it," said Sam, as if he had just heard her.

"No."

"The one that was opening at UFA-Palast." Sam caught the waitress's eye, made a circular motion in the air with his forefinger, indicating another round. Thea held one hand aloft, to let the waitress know she'd had enough.

"They're going to play *Wounded Germany* instead," she told him.

Sam repeated, *"Wounded Germany."* The logo on his new camera, Thea could see now, was Pathé-Baby. She had forgotten how useless he could be at times.

The waitress set down Sam's coffee, taking away the empty cup in a fluid circular motion. Thea looked behind her to the café's long wall which, she realized, was an enlarged photograph of the New York skyline, at night, which someone had shaded quite subtly with pastels. She recalled meeting Lang at the dock in Bremen, nine years ago now. He'd just arrived from New York City and could speak of nothing else. The lights, the architecture. As Lang described the city at night, Thea showed him some of her notes for her novel of the future, *Metropolis*. Lang, all Manhattan aslant in his mind, knew it must be a film, knew how that film must look.

Thea looked up to see Sam reading the March issue of *Black Mask*, mailed to him from the States. "There's a story in here," he told her, "which takes place in a film studio." He said it as if the coincidence were uncanny. The Zuntz windows were fitted with Venetian blinds, angled to protect the front tables from direct glare, and which only partially obscured any view of the street. A quartet of young boys in shorts and cloth caps was tossing a ball among themselves. The ball was large, air-filled, and the boys delighted in holding it over their heads before hurling it away.

" 'Mark Hull came out of the drugstore,' " Sam was saying in English, " 'got into his battered Ford coupé and drove down Sunset. He turned off on a side street, parked the Ford at the curb. He walked along a high cement wall with big signs advertising motion pictures on top of it. He walked past an iron gate with a khaki-uniformed policeman sitting on a stool beside it.' "

Mid-skyline Thea discerned the silhouette of the Chrysler Building, her favorite, for a few brief months in 1930 the world's tallest. She could not find the Empire State Building. The photo then would be almost exactly three years old. Slightly younger, she found herself thinking, than the boys in the street, who did not seem more than four. (She'd not swear to it, having been wildly wide of the mark, in the past, hazarding the age of children.) What, she wondered, had been the age of the blonde child, with whom she'd exchanged a long regard, in the stands at Nürburgring?

"That was Mark Hull," said Sam, speaking once again in his slow, methodical German. "Mark Hull entering a film studio. Isn't that a marvelous description?"

Her own child would have been just five. She'd had an abortion, in the summer of 1927, between *Spies* and *Woman in the Moon*. It had not been as painful as she had been led to believe it might. Dr. Humm had performed the surgery, and as far as she knew had not told Lang. It was before Lang refused to stop sleeping with others, long before she had felt able to sleep with anyone else; but she did not trust Lang to understand that this was not a child she wanted to bear. There was something in the secret between Thea and her dentist which enforced a sickening intimacy between them. She'd not allowed Humm since then to use anything stonger on her than local anæsthetic; and sometimes not even that.

Sam was saying, "The coffee is better in Paris," when the air-filled ball hit the window, splatting harmlessly. The child who had thrown it put a hand to his mouth. Then Thea became aware that Sam was once again recounting the tale of the Surrealist invasion of the Maldoror supper club. "Breton shouted repeatedly, 'We are the guests of Count Lautréamont,'" Sam told her. Char argued with the bouncer, Breton and Sam tore tablecloths away, flinging down plates, glasses, champagne buckets. "They called us names and tried to hit us, but they always missed. Eluard tried to convince the police that indeed it was *we* who had been attacked." He went on to describe Sadoul being thrown through a door, Char decking the bouncer. "Was that not a time?" Sam concluded. Thea hadn't been listening intently, but could make out no variation from the last time he'd told it. She looked toward the Chrysler Building.

"Shall we?" said Sam finally, signaling for the check, after neither had said anything for perhaps a minute. He cradled the camera, lens up. "My Pathé-Baby," he said.

Thea asked, "What happened to the old one?"

Sam smiled. "It got smashed in a riot."

Thea stood up, finding her view of the street obliterated slat by slat as she rose. Sam was standing too, camera in his left hand, *Black Mask* protruding from the back trouser pocket, title upward. Thea was sick of his sweaters. It had been quite a while since she had seen him sober; and she was not at all sure she preferred it.

133

He held the door for her. Outside he offered a Camel, which she fitted into the holder. The crowd which had gathered for the Mexican circus had all gone now. A fluffed cumulus cloud passed directly beneath the sun, imparting a nostalgic brown palette to the mortar and brickwork of the row houses across the wide street.

"Are you coming?" Sam asked.

Thea said, "I think not." It was the first time she could recall that they had met and parted without spending the night.

"Call me," said Sam, before turning.

Thea went left. To avoid retracing her steps and passing the Romanische entrance yet again, she could cross to the church, pass Ku-Damm on the left, and walk alongside the Zoological Garden. There was a cab stand, by the station, where she could rent transportation home. Left foot off the curb, Thea felt something hit the outside of her calf. One of the four-year-olds, hands crossed in front of him, made a face of contrition, held it. He assumed an extraordinary stillness as the soft, air-filled ball, in a parody of guilt, rolled slowly back toward him.

"Jurgen," said a woman's voice. Approaching from Nürnbergerstrasse, the woman advanced upon the frozen Jurgen, whose companions struck poses of elaborate disinterest. The woman, about Thea's age, wore a black wool coat of nubby bouclé. "Jurgen," the woman said, and then, "Thea?"

Thea looked at her as the pulpy ball, from whose trajectory there was no appeal, came to a stop directly at Jurgen's feet.

"Hanna Brant." It was a woman Thea had known somewhat at Luisen, well enough to nod to along the sunlit diagonal path which led to the dormitory. "Now Hanna Vogel," she was saying. Her face was overly animated, as if accustomed, from conversation with children, to broadly demonstrative gestures. She was clearly middle-aged.

Thea said, "Hanna." She did not know what had led her to think things with Sam would be different now. It made no sense. It was a wonder, really, that it had ever made sense.

"Schoolmate," said Hanna. Thea found herself at once worried that Hanna might be the tenacious sort, from whom it might be awkward to disengage. Thea looked down. One of Jurgen's playmates was gathering a fold of Hanna's coat within his curled fist.

Hanna said, "My Franz." Thea said hello. Franz put his face to his mother's coat; and then, losing interest, wandered off to rejoin his friends. They were dismantling, limb by limb, their detailed nonchalance. Then, as if cued, they resumed play.

"Tell Jurgen to apologize," Hanna said to her son, who seemed not to hear. "I've just come to fetch him," she told Thea. "We live in Alexanderplatz now." It was a working-class district of dreary tenements, whose social clubs Thea frequented from time to time. The district was dominated by the block-long police headquarters, familiarly called "Alex."

Thea heard herself say, "There was a Mexican circus right here, not an hour ago."

"It's been too long," Hanna said. She turned, and pronounced the name of her son.

"I like your coat," said Thea finally. Her own coat was perhaps fifteen years old. It was the one with Germany's lost provinces stitched into the lining.

"Thank you," said Hanna, turning toward her Franz, and saying his name several times.

"One moment," Franz said.

"Now," said Hanna.

Franz bade formal solemn good-bye to each of his playmates in turn. It recalled to Thea the receiving line at a diplomatic reception.

"Franz, say good-bye to Frau Lang." Thea hadn't mentioned her marriage, but it was silly to suppose it was something Hanna would not have heard, or read.

Franz said, "Good-bye," taking hold once more of his mother's coat. Thea said, "It was a pleasure meeting you, Franz. So long, Hanna."

"It's been too long," Hanna said again. They waved, and turned to find themselves walking off in the same direction. Hanna smiled.

Thea said, "It's always embarrassing."

At the corner of the Garden, Franz spotted a balloon vendor and, grabbing at the coats of the two women accompanying him, halted the procession.

"Let me buy him a balloon," said Thea finally. The balloon seller was quite tall, what was left of his hair cut close to the scalp. He wore dark glasses, and held his head in such a way it was possible to think him blind.

"The best one, for a very special boy," said Thea, handing him a large coin. Thea watched him work his fingers among the cords which converged in skeins, like perspective lines, at the handle of his cart.

To her right, near the gate, a squat man with a half-beard removed the end flap of a medium-sized parcel. With confusing flurry a pigeon which had been within that parcel took flight. Thea had seen the man before, on the top deck of a bus, when she'd been on her way from the vom Epoch; and again somewhere else, as well, that she couldn't quite recall now. Over the street noise, super-imposed on the Zoo Garden vista, Thea heard the words she had written for Peter Lorre, on trial before the gangster court. *But can I— Can I help it? Haven't I got this curse inside me? The fire? The voice? The pain? Again—again and again I have to walk the streets. And always I feel that somebody is following me— It is I myself. Following—me.*

"Say thank you," Hanna was telling Franz. The vendor detached a balloon from the cluster, held out its cord, which Franz took and wrapped around his wrist.

Franz said, "Thank you." Thea knew that she did not want to see Sam again; and that whatever had gone on between them was over now. She walked slowly, allowing Hanna and Franz to forge ahead toward Zoo Station. Hanna was holding the neck of the balloon. Her child dangled behind her, appended by perhaps two meters of a string. It recalled for Thea the way Martini Szeny had dangled from the length of chain, as the gray-suited man on the motorcycle—truly Szeny's brother?—had let slip the clutch.

S I X

LANG WAS TYPING AGAIN. THEA HAD ONCE asked him to put padding between his machine and the hard surface of his desk; but he'd told her he was quite pleased with the height of the thing, and afraid any padding would make it too high. He liked his forearms parallel with the floor. Now the snapping came from behind his closed door in a rage of productivity. She'd inquired several times whether she might see his "Viennese confection," as he'd come to refer to it. He said only that he was loath to show it before it was finished.

The last scenario he'd written alone was *Spiders*. It had concerned a secret society bent on world domination, whose efforts were continually thwarted by the handsome adventurer Kai Hoog. Hoog, chased by a cohort of Spiders, grabs the dangling ballast cord of an ascending balloon, floating to safety. "Flee," says the Princess of the Incas to Hoog: "Death awaits you here." But it is not in Kai Hoog's character to flee. Hoog never looks happier than when announcing, "I have arranged a raid on the suspected house."

The Spiders are led by Lio Sha, who wears mannish double-breasted jackets over her comfortable belly. Lio Sha is, of course, madly in love with Hoog; and when Hoog spurns her for the love of the Princess of the Incas, the fate of the innocent Princess is sealed. Later, entering the subterranean city—a Spider stronghold accessible only through a concealed entrance somewhere in Chinatown—Hoog can be seen to say, "I have an old score to settle."

Thea had some small affection for *Spiders*. But somehow she did not think her husband's "Viennnese confection" a scenario of that sort. Sitting before her circular mirror now, Thea supposed he'd want to do something more "meaningful," make a "statement." She drew two long arches, in soft pencil, at the top of her eyebrows. Hoog had been nowhere near as interesting as his portly mannish nemesis. (She supposed Hoog the first in a long line of hapless prosecutors.) Lifting her gaze up and to the right, Thea sensed movement in the corner of her mirror. She refocused to see Lang walking toward her. The buttons on his double-breasted mirror jacket were fastened right over left, Lio Sha style. Thea hadn't noticed, but the typing must have stopped while she'd been thinking. As he approached his head became lost over the edge of the mirror. Then he was behind her, his hand on her shoulder.

"Thea."

There was a gold band on the fourth finger of the hand which rested on her shoulder. It was his left hand, but did not appear so in the mirror, where it looked wrong.

"You are applying makeup," he told her.

Thea said lightly, "I can see no point in denying it." She smiled, not knowing if Lang could see her expression from where she stood.

"In preparation for your American?"

Thea turned to look at him directly. He backed off a few paces, then sat abruptly as the edge of the bed clipped him at the knees. Taking hold of the sides of her bench, Thea swiveled to face him.

"No," she told him, and then added, "But how sweet of you to ask."

"This is no joking matter," he said, hands clasped in his lap, back maddeningly erect. She had a dinner date, with Klein-Rogge; but she was not at all sure she wanted to let Lang know it was "only" her ex-husband.

"I'm not joking," she told him finally.

Lang said, "Good."

Thea reached for a teardrop-shaped crystal bottle of polish remover. She could finish the eyebrows later.

"We must talk," he said, tugging at the trouser fabric just above his knees. Rudolf had invited her to dine at the Scala with Correll. He said the studio was having trouble with its summer schedule, as much established talent had decided to leave Germany; and that Correll wished to sound her out about whether she'd be willing to direct.

Lang was tugging at an earlobe. "You promise that you're not off to a rendezvous with Sam?"

The odor of polish remover began to permeate the air, tropical, oversweet. He'd put some emphasis on the last word. Thea tried to recall whether she'd ever used Sam's name in front of her husband. She did not think she had.

She said, "I will not be interrogated."

Lang rose, took four steps, sat down beside her. Thea finished up her left hand, and was at work on the right, with a fresh ball of cotton.

He lit a Boyard, returned the matches to his pocket.

Cigarette in his lips, Lang took up the faceted polish remover bottle, seemed to be considering it. Then he pulled his arm back, in a hurling motion, and let fly the bottle, toward the circular vanity mirror.

It hit, just off-center.

A network of cracks bloomed outward from the point of impact. More lines appeared, finer now; and then concentric circles, which intersected the initial radiating faults in the manner of a spider's web.

A few of the larger triangular segments detached themselves from the mirror and fell, hitting the vanity and the floor.

There was a great clatter. More pieces fell, and some of the adjoining segments, still affixed, buckled a bit, reflecting new portions of the room.

The bottle hit the small rug at Thea's feet with a muffled, dense thud, bouncing once. Then it came to rest. One of the larger pieces of mirror had landed on her lap, its point just piercing the black dress, taut between her thighs.

Many parts of the mirror were no longer there, replaced by blank unreflecting wall. Others were now off-vertical; still others crazed to opacity. Thea could see one of her husband's eyes afloat in a sea of unrecognizable image. Another segment, above it and to its left, reflected his forearm. Then she could make out her own face, off to the side. She watched her own eyes fill up, a regard she maintained with some ferocity until tears blurred her vision. She blinked several times, and was able to see her pale blue eyes once more.

"I've stopped seeing him," she told Lang. Thea turned away from the shatter toward her husband, who had fashioned a mask of contrition not unlike that of the small boy, Jurgen, whose ball had hit her on the calf Wednesday on Tauentzienstrasse. Yet the corners of Lang's mouth were curling upward, in what she took as an expression of victory.

He said, "Yes?" Then he closed his mouth, compressing his lips frightfully.

Thea put her face to her hands.

"I'm sorry," Lang told her.

She could not look at him. Regarding the shards around her vanity Thea told him, "Get out."

She listened to him walk away in regular heavy steps, one of which was accompanied by a crunch, as of broken glass, to which Lang, in thick-soled bluchers, seemed not to pay heed. She was glad she'd not applied her eye makeup, because she would have to redraw all now, after tears. Klein-Rogge had talked of a project which UFA had intended to hand Robert Siodmak, who hung out in the "swimming pool" room at the Romanische, and who had worked with Ulmer, Billy Wilder, Zinnemann, and Schufftan on *People on Sunday*. This week Siodmak had emigrated to Paris.

Thea heard the latch click home as her husband shut the door behind him. Tomorrow she would find out how much longer she would have to wait before reoccupying Dahlem. It would be such a relief, to be in the country, on her own, with the dogs and cats. Outside twilight was giving way to night. The overhead at once seemed brighter and Thea became aware of distinct beams of light, reflected upward off scattered fragments of mirror. The beams pierced the room at oblique angles, like spotlights at a premiere.

There was a knocking sound, accompanied by Lang's voice, from the other side of the door. "We must talk," he was saying. Thea, in slippers, stepped carefully away from the mirror. The rip in her dress was quite small, but Thea thought it best to change into a new one, after she had dealt with the man on the other side of the door.

She opened it, walked past him to the dining room table. Lang took a seat opposite. He offered a cigarette, which she declined. She watched him light up, and vowed to get through this conversation without tobacco. It would really be best, she knew, not to have a cigarette until she was out of the apartment. She could light up by the guard gate, while waiting for Josef to fetch her a cab.

"You must warn Sam," said Lang without preface.

Thea studied the Otto Dix portraits of herself, which she felt, of late, more comfortable with than she had when they were just painted. Lang's absurd Incan raven was still perched on the mantel.

"The police spoke with me," he went on.

Thea said, "The vanity mirror you destroyed belonged to my mother, and is not replaceable."

Lang, looking pale and in need of a shave, said, "They showed me photographs and film." His voice was flat, weary, as if explaining something for the fourth or fifth time. "They have been following him."

" 'How little do people suspect death stalks their foot-steps.' " Thea found herself replying: " 'That their lives are as brief as that of the rose.' " It was something she'd written for one of their earlier films, although she could not recall which one at the moment. She smiled, that in a discussion about Sam she'd lapsed into quotation.

"You must warn him," Lang was saying.

Thea noticed a large shard of vanity mirror she'd apparently carried, in her hand, from the bedroom. "Why,"

Thea asked, "the sudden concern?" She went to her pocketbook, came up with a nail file, with which she began to scrape at the silvering. It came off the back of the fragment with surprising ease, leaving an ashy residue on the table.

"They've been following him day and night. The political police. They said that at a word from me they'd have him picked up."

Thea had decided to remove the silvering from perhaps half the shard. She adjusted the pressure so the file would not squeak against glass. Then she held it up, to see her husband's face through the clear portion and, in the reflective half, her own.

"And you didn't give the word?" Thea said finally.

During the filming of Metropolis the special-effects cinematographer Eugen Schufftan had devised a process to combine live action with miniature representations of scenery. He did it by scraping off part of a mirror's silvering, placing the thing at a forty-five-degree angle to the lens axis. The live action was shot through the scraped half, miniature sets, off to the side, reflected in the untouched remainder. She'd had no trouble grasping the concept. The workings of a film set were no mystery to her, as they would be to most women.

"No," Lang was saying, regarding his hands. "No."

Thea laid the mirror on the table with a satisfying snap, as if placing the ultimate piece of a jigsaw puzzle.

Lang lit another cigarette and said, "They're serious."

Thea smiled.

"They spoke of a police record in Paris," he went on.

She said, "You call him." She rose. "I have to change."

Lang remained seated, busying himself with the cigarette.

"Would you have told me all this about Sam, had I not let you know I was no longer seeing him?"

The sick-dog look played briefly across Lang's face, replaced by his familiar contemplative gaze. He removed his monocle, tapping it against the piece of mirror Thea had left on the table. Then he walked over to the fireplace, and spread kindling across the andiron grate.

He took two logs, placed them at a small angle atop the kindling.

Thea said, " 'Jealousy is as cruel as the grave—' "

" '—and the coals thereof are as coals of fire,' " Lang joined in, and they spoke in slow-cadenced unison: " 'which burn with a vehement flame.' " It was the epigraph card to *Destiny*. Thea was surprised that Lang could recall it after all these years.

He held a match to the kindling, which burst into light. His kneeling shadow was long against the parquet flooring, reaching out to where Thea stood.

"A group of artists didn't like the name of a night-club. They showed up without reservations and cried a lot until they got themselves beat up. The next day they sat at the outdoor café, displaying their wounds to female pass-ersby. That's the police record in Paris," Thea said.

Lang, still bent over the hearth, made a sound in his throat; and though she could not see his face, Thea supposed him to be laughing. She would wear the black velvet dress, whose sleeves came down halfway to the wrist.

The Tiller Girls were clad for this number in top hats and stylized versions of men's cutaways, in sateen. They kicked high, in unison, arms around one another, across the length of the Scala's stage, now lit deep red, deep blue. Correll had secured one of the better tables, just behind the first semicircular railing. It was raised perhaps half a meter above the main flooring, enabling them to see over the heads of the enthusiastic crowd below. Thea watched tendrils of smoke twist and twirl in dramatic cones of spotlight. Klein-Rogge and Correll were drinking cognac, Thea coffee. Her ex-husband was also toying with a large slice of chocolate cake, iced in hazelnut butter cream.

"Already gone," Correll was saying. "Both Siodmaks, in fact." He counted on his fingers. "Wilder, Ophuls." Klein-Rogge had steered the conversation to the emigration problem. "Schufftan, just today," Correll went on.

"Thea and I worked with him on *Metropolis*," Klein-Rogge said. He was wearing brilliantine, and the hair just below the exquisitely drawn part glinted deep blue in the spotlight. The Tiller Girls had split up into groups of four and were performing precision whirls, emulating the hypnotic spiral of hundreds of tiny electric bulbs, center stage.

"The Jews seem to be loaning themselves out to Paris," said Correll. Thea found herself thinking once more about Hanna, her classmate, whom she'd run into outside the Zuntz. Several times today Thea replayed their encounter, though she'd paid little attention to it at the time.

"I fancy the third one from the left," Klein-Rogge was telling Correll, who raised a glass and replied, "Shall we discover her?"

"Perhaps later," said Klein-Rogge, with a glance toward his former wife.

It had something to do, Thea realized now, with Hanna's face. Hanna had not gotten grossly fat; and there was nothing peremptorily hideous in those lines which fifteen years of care had engraved. Yet it was only one of the multitude of faces which the girl Thea knew in convent school could have come to own. There was something in those lost faces, never to be seen now, which Thea found painfully moving, though there was certainly no reason for it. She tried to image some of the "other" faces; but the real one kept reappearing before her mind's eye, dispelling all else. Thea wondered how she could have gotten to this point without having acquired any friends to speak of, save perhaps ludicrous Ilsa, and Klein-Rogge who, as her ex-husband, did not count.

"I once had some success," Correll was saying, "with an Admiral Girl."

"I'm sure you offered her a job, as an extra in *Metropolis*," Klein-Rogge replied.

Correll said, "That's very funny."

"I remember her in the crowd scenes," the actor said.

Twenty silver Tiller Girls, in a line, raised linked arms, allowing twenty gilt-clad sisters to come through. The audience applauded loudly.

"How is your husband's scenario going?" Correll was asking. Lang hadn't mentioned discussing the project with UFA; but he wouldn't necessarily have told her.

Thea said, "He's working very hard."

"Has he talked to you about it?" Correll held a lighter to her cigarette. Klein-Rogge seemed absorbed in the stage show. "No," said Thea finally.

"It seems a bit sentimental to me," said Correll. "Old-fashioned. Perhaps not in the best sense of that word."

The gold and silver Tiller Girls, intermingled now, were marching downstage. "It's a shame," Correll went on, "that he works so hard on a Saturday night."

Thea said nothing.

Onstage, masses of dry-ice fog were seeping in, to cover the appearance of a set of Jessner stairs, center stage, Painted clouds scudded across the blue-lit cyclorama. As if at once, the Tiller Girls had sprouted angel wings. Draped in more fog than she would have believed possible, the girls climbed upward, with much fluttering of translucent wings. As they reached the top of the stairs they seemed to disappear into the clouds. Correll was swirling his cognac. Blue and white highlights off the rim of his glass left faint afterimage trails against the club's unlit wall. "Have you given any thought," he asked, "to directing?"

Klein-Rogge, whose regard of the ascending Tiller Girls remained unbroken, displayed his good profile. She was not successful in attempts to catch his eye.

Correll said, "On a Saturday night," in a lower, more guttural tone, no longer pitched to carry above the orchestra. "Your husband," Correll added, "must be a fool." Thea began to stub her cigarette, then took another drag. She did not want to bring her forearm within range of Correll's fingers, not just now.

"Rudolf! Tell Thea what a fool Lang must be, to neglect her so shamelessly!"

Klein-Rogge turned away from the Tiller spectacle, looking small and lost. He drained his glass, essaying a smile.

"It would be an honor," Thea said finally, "to direct for UFA." She wondered what her own face looked like in this light, and whether there were other faces which could have been hers, but which she had not come to own. It was silly to think about. Correll was counting on his fingers again, ticking off the departed Jews, one by one.

The stairs themselves were being elevated by an unseen winch: and the clouds, on fine-wire guys, were now passing in front of the Tiller Girls as well as behind them. The light on the cyclorama was a serene pale blue, picked up by the gold and silver reflective angels. The Tiller Girls were waving good-bye now. Correll extended a leather cigar case to Klein-Rogge, who waved it away. Correll took one, preparing the end with a small brass nipping engine. It had a diagonal blade. The amputated tip flew up in the air, landed on the tablecloth.

"In celebration," said Correll, lighting up. He held the wax match some distance below the tip of the cigar, which he rotated until it was evenly lighted. Thea knew at once that she must find Sam, and let him know he was in danger of arrest if he did not leave Berlin.

"No one could direct me better than Thea," said Klein-Rogge abruptly. His eyes had not left the stage.

Thea said, "I must go."

There was a good deal of sweat on Klein-Rogge's upper lip as he permitted a relieved smile to break across his face.

"The finale," said Correll, detaining Thea's forearm. Tiller Girls, from the very top of the proscenium arch, were scattering rose petals onto the audience.

Klein-Rogge said quickly, "May I show you home?"

"The foolish Herr Lang," said Correll finally, almost to himself. White spotlights hit the revolving mirror ball. Small stars of light floated around the walls and tables.

"We can speak at your office Monday?" Thea said to Correll, briefly covering his hand with her own.

"That will be delightful." He was composed now, taking stock of his cigar. One spotlight remained on the mirror ball as others roved the audience, cutting swaths of frenzy.

Thea stood up.

"This scene begs," said Correll, gesturing grandly, "for an overhead camera."

"You are quite right," said Klein-Rogge. He made to stand.

Thea said, "I can see myself to a cab." A spotlight hit her full in the face, harsh whiteness obliterating all features, save hair and eyes. She reeled blindly, in a confusion of afterimage. Somehow Klein-Rogge had gotten ahead of her, leading the way toward the coat check. He stopped, putting his chin on her shoulder, to be heard over the orchestra, the din of celebration. "Fritz treats you well?" he asked.

His hands were in a half-clench, as if prepared to do battle. He backed off, patting the hair at the side of his head, just behind the temple. Then he was hit by the light, momentarily bleached out. Overexposed, his face seemed unformed, shockingly young; and then very old.

"Quite well," Thea told him.

Klein-Rogge took the coat check ticket from her hand, regarding it intently. "When the car gets bogged down," he said finally, "who is to dig it out? In human relations I mean."

Thea lit a match whose flame was rendered invisible in the grand sweep of spotlight.

*　　*　　*

Thea was glad she'd worn the black wool coat: in the half-sleeved velvet dress she was far too formal for the Zuntz. A man at the front table looked up from his unshaven perusal of *Le Figaro* and stared until she shut the door behind her. Once more she found herself the only woman in the house, excepting the waitress. Sam preferred the rear, away from the windows; but he was not there now. Thea always found the Zuntz somewhat depressing on weekend nights. There was a phone in the back from which she could once more try the vom Epoch.

"Thea?"

The man—quite tall, quite thin—was seated by the wall, just beneath the hand-tinted lights of Manhattan's downtown financial district. He wore a short mustacheless beard. His face was not unfamiliar.

"Will you join me?" he said in accented German. Thea unbuttoned her coat without removing it. She pulled out a chair, hoping to recall who this man was before the conversation took a turn which would force her to ask, or expose her ignorance.

"A chocolate," Thea told the waitress.

The man's cigarette, which he'd been about to light, was quite loosely packed. Coarse, dark tobacco spilled out the end. "How have you been?" she asked finally.

"No complaints," said the man, igniting a kitchen match with his thumbnail in a gesture which brought back to her the man's name: Antonio. He was a friend of Sam whom they'd run into at a boxing match just before Christmas. He'd given Sam the addresses of some architects in Barcelona, and some specific regards he wished Sam to convey. "I just come here," he went on, "before retiring. I live a mere three blocks away, and it is convenient for me to take my nightcap here." Then his cigarette went out, and he was relighting it. Nothing specific, but she assumed him to be homosexual.

"You haven't seen Sam?" She worked hard to keep her voice flat and was quite pleased with how it came out, just this side of nonchalance. She looked up and to the right, toward the Chrysler Building's towering spire. The first time she'd had occasion to put the word on paper she'd written "Kreisler," which for some reason had entertained Lang no end.

"I saw *The Anthem of Leuthen* at the Palast with a friend, and just stopped off here on my way home." He sipped from the brandy glass in front of him.

"Did you like it?" Thea heard herself say. There was a great sputter of steamed milk from the counter.

Antonio recrossed his legs and said, "You're the second person to ask."

Thea fitted a Camel into her holder—Sam's brand, it occurred to her now, though she'd given it no thought, plucking the pack from the tray which the cigarette girl held in front of her, at the Scala. Now she found herself studying the minarets and onion towers on the pack's obverse. Perhaps after the assignment he had in mind for her Correll would let her direct something of her own, perhaps even the North African project, which swirled in her mind like wind over sand.

"A very popular man tonight," Antonio went on. Thea recalled *Kwan-Yin*, a story about a Chinese princess she'd written during the filming of the first *Mabuse* in 1922. Somehow the project had gotten lost, and they'd found themselves at work on the *Nibelungen*. She was sure she could take the old story and Arabicize it—East to Near East—without much trouble.

Antonio was saying, "He asked the barman whether Sam had been in tonight."

"Yes," said Thea. She'd not been following.

"About Sam," Antonio said. Thea, who had been gazing off toward the Queensboro Bridge, returned her regard abruptly to the Spaniard. He was scratching his beard, which resembled a chin strap.

"Who?" said Thea, as it began to register.

"A scar down his cheek. The kind they all claim to have gotten from dueling, in Heidelberg." Antonio knocked back most of what was left in his glass.

"How long ago?"

"I don't spend my evenings here." He signaled for another brandy. Thea realized she'd not gotten her chocolate. "Don't you listen? I was at the films, with a friend." His long arms were waving about in frenetic semaphore. "I only stop here for a nightcap, because it is convenient to my home."

Thea looked at him.

"About fifteen minutes before your arrival," Antonio said finally. "He asked the barman whether Sam Harrison had been in tonight. The barman said no."

The waitress—not the same one as yesterday—set down chocolate and a brandy. There were two empty glasses on the table in addition to the one just set down, and the one in his hand, not quite finished.

"That's the whole thing," Antonio said.

Thea added sugar from a hinge-lidded chrome-plated bowl. They had been filming *Anthem* at UFA in December. It was the latest in the Frederick the King series. She'd watched them shoot one scene where the King, on the eve of battle, debates setting aside funds for cultural purposes, "to strengthen our nation."

Antonio was saying, "You might try the Forget-Me-Not." He leaned into her face, the air between them sharp with alcohol and garlic. The man was not homosexual, not at all. In fact there was some baroque story about Antonio and a girl far younger than he which had ended in Andalusian scandal. It was a story Sam had told her the night of the boxing match, but the details were escaping her just now. She watched Antonio remove a shred of tobacco which had gotten stuck to his tongue. Forget-Me-Not was a club near Alexanderplatz where one could get drugs, and which remained open well after hours.

"Thanks," Thea said finally. She buttoned her coat, then rummaged in her pocketbook to pay for the chocolate, which she'd hardly touched.

Antonio said, "I seem to be a bit short tonight," jerkily waving his arm across the array of snifters.

"Yes. Well." She took a note from her wallet, placing it on the table, smoothing out creases with the side of her palm. It was Saturday, the eleventh of March. Two years ago exactly, F. W. Murnau had died in a car crash in California. Thea had, at one point, written a scenario for him, *Burning Soil*; and she had no reservations about the way he'd filmed it. She and Murnau had been born on adjacent days, the week after Christmas, 1888.

The cab took her along Tiergarten's southern edge. It was a route she'd traveled hundreds of times, and she'd always taken special pleasure in it. As a young girl, on her rare visits to Berlin, she'd close her eyes, evoking a sense of dark, palpable respiration off to her left, in the park's nocturnal depths, where the nighttime bears did the gavotte. She would explain to Father why you could never catch sight of the bears past daybreak, and tell him of the clandestine hiding holes where they went when humans were around; but he would never believe her, and she would have to explain it once more. "Why," he would ask finally, "did the bears decide to let *you* in on their little secret?"

"Because," she said aloud now, in the cab's rear seat, the unlit Philharmonic Hall off to the right. "Because."

Now they turned briefly into the park. Her eyes acclimated to the darkness; and the Brandenburg Gate loomed in front of them, all hard edges, harsh shadows. It was lit, as if for filming, from below, by six huge blue-white arc lamps. Thea thought of the nighttime bears, her old friends, no use to her now. Under the gate, where the arc lamps did not reach, the darkness outside turned window to mirror. She saw herself, some overdressed adventuress. The dark pursuit of a reckless American, himself tracked mercilessly by the scar-faced stranger. Down Unter den Linden now, where there was at this hour almost no other traffic. Two headlights, about a block behind them. They made a left at Saint Hedwig's, a right on Rathausstrasse, traveling northeast now, nothing in the oval rear window as far as she could tell. Thea thought about her own face, and the face of the adventuress which she could study, in melodramatic half-light, superimposed on the receding scenery, just the other side of the rear window. She felt at once quite alone in the world, in a way she had not for some years. Alone, and very far from home. In this sector the Spree splits for a couple of kilometers; and on Rathausstrasse they had to cross it twice. She found herself grateful for the forward motion of the cab. As long as it bore her ahead there was nothing she could do to get there faster, or to make things any different.

She had the cab let her off at Alexanderplatz, just across Münzstrasse from the police headquarters, overtipping the driver, rare for her. She stood there as he pulled away. An enormous number of lights were still on in the red brick headquarters, not surprising when she considered it. They'd taken her on a tour of Alex when she'd been writing M. She had been particularly fascinated by the fine-ground silver dust, which they used to develop latent fingerprints; and, of course, by the Pigeon Board. Now, walking away from the headquarters toward the Forget-Me-Not, she recalled the familiar-looking half-bearded man who'd released a pigeon from a parcel, as she'd bought the balloon for young Franz. It had not quite occurred to her, at the time, that the man must have been a member of the Pigeon Squad; and Thea wondered now if the man had been following her, or perhaps Sam. She thought of the places she'd been in the past week, imagined them at once as they would look in a scattered lattice of yellow pins, on the enormous street plan. She could almost see one of Commander Friedrich's little men holding, as a tailor, pins between his teeth, at the ready. Waiting for the next sighting of subject von Harbou, hoping half-aloud that she stayed within Central Berlin. (The map man, on the day she'd been given the tour, had muttered oaths for those under surveillance who stayed south, forcing him to his knees; and for those who ran north, toward Wedding, necessitating the dark-wood stepladder.)

A police car, then another, passed her now, presumably returning to Alex. There were no other cars. On Königstrasse her heels struck the cobbles with a high, flinty click which came back at her in syncopation from the building frontage.

Midway between two lamps Thea cast shadows of equal length before and behind. The shadow in front of her elongated, became more vague, as she approached the next lamp. The echo seemed to come back fractionally later than she'd been anticipating, and she stopped, to see if there were another set of footsteps dogging her own; but there were not.

Thea found herself reciting half-audibly the words she'd written for Peter Lorre: *again and again I have to walk the streets.* She fashioned the words into a rhythm which fit comfortably with her footsteps.

On each side were six-story working-class tenements, twenty-four horrid railroad flats in each. It occurred to her now that one of them belonged to Hanna, her classmate, and the small boy Franz. Perhaps the blonde child from Nürburgring lived here as well. She was more than half-way to the corner.

It was quite humid, and mist gave shape to the cones of light beneath the streetlamps, the way cigarette smoke, she was reminded, will give form to the beam of a film projector.

Abruptly she saw herself as if from a great distance, moving at slow pace down the grid of Alexanderplatz's narrow, regular streets. She was unsure for a moment whether she was in Berlin, or a map of Berlin. Whether she was moving herself down Königstrasse or was being moved, by some minor functionary, implanting yellow pins on a vertical street plan.

Thea took fifteen steps with eyes closed. When she opened them she was quite near the corner. She lengthened her stride to reach the corner more quickly, without being heard to accelerate. She turned the corner and exhaled.

The metal door to the Forget-Me-Not was crossed by four lengths of wood planking nailed to the frame. A hand-lettered piece of cardboard, tacked to one of the planks, said simply:

CLOSED BY THE POLICE

It was not clear whether the notice had been posted by the club's owners or the police themselves. Thea rested a palm against the door which was cold and somewhat wet with condensation. She placed her forehead against the door. Thea heard herself saying *again and again,* in the walking rhythm, surprised to find she was still reciting it. After a while Thea removed her forehead, cold now, from the metal door with a sideways peeling motion. She wondered if there had been a raid, and if Sam had gotten caught up in it.

Looking north she saw a well-lit broad intersection which, if she remembered correctly, would be Prenzlauerstrasse. She made for it, swinging her arms in wide arcs as if strolling. It was five minutes past one.

At the Prenzlauerstrasse corner there was a concrete advertising pillar, half again as tall as Thea. It was covered with countless layers of posters and notices, and bellied out in the middle where, over the months, most of the notices had been pasted. Behind one torn corner Thea saw an advertisement for Otto Reuter at the Kaffee Zielke. He hadn't performed there, she was sure, since last November.

A poster advertised the forthcoming *Wounded Germany*, opening soon at UFA-Palast. Down the margin, in red grease pencil:

$$
\frac{\dfrac{\begin{array}{c}12\\9\\14\\11\end{array}}{31}}{\begin{array}{c}1\\5\end{array}}
$$

It was cocaine dealers' shorthand, which she'd learned while writing *Spies*. The first section spelled out the name of the street by ordinal number: 1 = A, 2 = B, etc. The second gave the street number, and lastly, the hours. Drugs would be available at 31 Linkstrasse from one to five.

Thea knew she had been meant to see the vertical red message. That she had been meant, as well, to understand it. She would not have been brought to this place otherwise. Sam was at 31 Linkstrasse. He'd have just gotten there. She could find him, warn him.

She would tell him to flee north, off the grid, where Friedrich's little man could not reach, even with the dark-wood stepladder; or perhaps south, to some distant sun-drenched land, such as the one which had served as model for the design on the back of the package of Sam's exclusive brand of cigarettes. In the sky to the west now Thea saw an illuminated X against lowering clouds. She took it as the trace of upward-aimed arc lights, at the base of the Brandenburg Gate.

Then the tenement frontage to her right brightened. Spinning around, Thea caught sight of a cab turning the corner. It was of a similar model to the one in which she had come to this working-class district. She extended an arm. The cab's headlights swept Prenzlauerstrasse, hitting the advertising pillar, the shadow of which spun across the intersection. Now the cab was stopped in front of her. It did not appear to have the same driver.

"Thirty-one Linkstrasse," she told him.

The cab executed a U-turn, heading toward Rosenthalerplatz, perhaps ten blocks distant. Linkstrasse, if she recalled correctly, was just the other side.

The cab's passenger compartment smelled of damp wool, and of cigars, as if a second- or third-class railway coach. Idly Thea fingered her coat lining, the embroidered emblems of the lost provinces.

They negotiated Rosenthalerplatz. The cab slowed. To the left, at the first corner, two cars parked lengthwise blocked the cross street.

Four uniformed policemen leaned against the cars or adjacent to them. One was lighting a pipe. There were two other men at the roadblock who wore the brown uniform of the SA. One of them held an electric torch which he swung in lazy counterclockwise circles, commanding the traffic to move on. It was not Linkstrasse. Linkstrasse was two blocks farther down.

The cab had no difficulty turning right onto the commencement of Linkstrasse. Thea heard police klaxons some blocks away which did not seem to be coming any closer.

Beginning with number 19, and extending almost to the end of the block, was a dirt lot. The next standing house was numbered 45, and it was boarded up. Thea made the driver back up and and go around the block once more, to be sure she'd not read the numbers incorrectly.

The demolition seemed fairly recent. (The ground, she noticed, had not yet been tramped down to uniform level.) The note on the advertising kiosk had been a lie, perhaps weeks out of date. She had known that Sam would be awaiting her at 31 Linkstrasse; and now could only think that the red-pencil markings had been a ruse to draw her here, away from some main action. Sam's enemies, knowing her power, had contrived to mislead her at a crucial moment. She should have known that the Spaniard was not to be trusted.

"Breitenbachplatz," Thea said finally, giving the driver her address. She would call the vom Epoch as soon as she got home, giving her name, in case he'd managed to leave a message for her.

As they turned onto Unter den Linden the driver said, "I hear there were one hundred fifty thousand in Lustgarten."

"Yes?" said Thea, recalling the announcements of a workers' rally at which, Dr. Goebbels would speak.

"One hundred fifty thousand," said the driver, who lapsed into silence until they had reached her building.

Josef the night man opened the cab door. Thea paid the driver. There were no messages for her at the desk.

She walked up the stairs recalling an old line of Lang's, that they had never managed to shoehorn into a film: "It is a night for evil spirits, and the prayers of unloved maidens." It would have made a splendid title card. The stairwell was dank, airless, but nowhere near as foul as the cab had been, even after Thea had cranked down the windows.

Inside Thea removed her black wool coat. She hung it in the closet, placing it carefully so it would not rub the coat adjacent. Circling the living room she ended up on the the rug, before the fire, legs folded beneath her. The coals were still aglow and she got up once to place a fresh log on the grate, hoping it would catch. She did not want to fuss with bellows, and kindling. She kicked off her shoes. Faint, intermittent typing sounds emerged from Lang's room. It was just past two. The hearth's warmth seemed to dispell the volatile memories of the way she had felt in the working-class district. Perhaps she'd not been tracing Sam's footsteps at all, but pursuing rather a trail of her own devise. Standing she poured out a glass of brandy, feeling at once quite inane. One might as well, she told herself now, imagine a subterranean city, accessed by false-front elevator, hidden behind a rack of curios in the rear room of an antique shop, in the Chinese district. That secret city, coextensive with Berlin, one kilometer beneath, inhabited by the criminal element, members of arcane societies, and those without proper motives.

"Thea?"

Lang came through the door to his room. He was wearing the red silk moiré robe, faded now to a burnished domestic crimson. He'd not shaved for quite some while. There was a pronounced purple crease at the side of his nose where the monocle had been.

"I'm finished," he said quietly. He went back to his room, emerged a moment later clutching a sheaf of papers perhaps four millimeters thick. He held the manuscript above his head, shaking it twice. It was a gesture Thea had never seen from her husband, one that belonged, rather, to a boxer at the bell of some late round when it becomes clear his opponent will not emerge from the far corner. Grinning with some ferocity, Lang placed the thing upon the living room table, giving it a small tap as if to hold it in place.

He said, *"The Legend of the Last Viennese Fiaker,"* and sat down. After a while he let go a short exultant cry; then his arms and neck went limp, all spent, against the leather chair.

"Congratulations."

"I just finished," he told her, in a tone which suggested it surprised him. Thea knew it would be hard to tell him that she wanted to take the Dix portraits with her when she returned to Dahlem. It was a discussion she did not look forward to.

"Could you fix me some cocoa?" Lang was saying, knees pulled up to his chest now.

Thea took three steps toward the kitchen.

The telephone began to ring.

"I'll get it," said Thea quite loudly, after several rings.

Lang, unmoving, said nothing. She walked deliberately to the bedroom, closing the door behind her. The phone was on the far side of the night table. She walked toward the bed swiftly, then dived, belly first, across. Picking up the receiver she said, "Sam?" It occurred to her that there was probably a fair amount of broken glass still hidden in the rug; and that she should have stepped more carefully, in her stocking feet.

"Thea," said the voice, which was not Sam's.

"Speaking," she said finally, when she had gotten hold of her breath.

The man on the telephone said, "I had to tell them."

"Who is this?" said Thea.

"Doctor Humm. I had to tell them. They threatened to revoke my license."

Thea rolled over onto her side, the phone wire winding about her.

"My practice," Humm was saying.

Thea said, "When—" but found herself interrupted. Humm said, "I can't talk now." There were several loud clicks. The line went dead.

She replaced the receiver, disentangling herself with some care from the phone cord. Then she dialed the number of the Hotel vom Epoch from memory.

Asking for Sam Harrison, she was told by the deskman after a minute's pause that Herr Harrison was indeed still registered, but was not in his room at the moment. "Tell him that Thea called," she said, spelling her first name. The deskman inquired if there were any message.

"No." She replaced the receiver gently. It was Saturday night, Sunday morning really, and he was neither with her nor in his room. It occurred to her that he was with another woman. She had not thought about Sam and other women since she had been seeing him; and now that it was over, it seemed quite silly to be upset by that kind of thought. Her gaze strayed from the fingernails of her left hand, past the ruined mirror to the door. She could not understand why she was so angry. Thea scanned the carpet, looking for shattered glass.

In the kitchen Lang had tied an apron over his robe, and was stirring a pan of milk which he'd placed on low heat over the burner. He'd put several spoons of cocoa into a cup, leaving a trail of brown powder across an expanse of countertop.

"It may be the best thing I've done," he said.

"Correll had his doubts," she found herself replying, and was immediately sorry that she'd done so. She waited for her husband to launch into interrogation, demanding a verbatim report of what Correll had said. Instead Lang said, "Correll can eat shit," with no particular vehemence. He took the handle in both hands, pouring carefully.

"Nebenzal has money. I have money. UFA can take it up the ass."

He was crushing lumps of cocoa with the bottom of his spoon against the sides of the cup. "UFA is composed of pigs and whoremongers," he went on absently.

Holding cup and saucer in front of him at chest level, Lang walked toward the living room. Thea followed. He set the cup down, returned to the kitchen, came back with the sugar. She wondered at what hour the Zuntz closed, and whether it would make sense to leave a message for Sam there as well.

Lang smiled and said, "Pigs." The log which Thea had placed on the hearth when she'd come in was burning well now, lazy flames licking around its sides. Thea heard a police siren outside, growing higher in pitch, louder; and then another.

Thea seated herself on the rug at her husband's feet, resting her back against his shins. They were both looking into the hearth. She felt his hand atop her head, patting abstractedly. She wondered if there were anything she could say that her husband would be pleased to hear. "May I read it?" she asked finally.

Lang said, "When it's retyped." She could not see his face as he said it.

The sirens were nearer, and there seemed at least three of them now. Lang took his hand away abruptly, as if at once aware of what he'd been doing. Thea was no longer seeing "another man," and did not know how to convince her husband that his rage had no use now.

Lang crossed his legs. Thea stood up. She walked toward the French doors which opened upon their little orator's balcony. The sirens were quite loud. Then the curtains were swept by an intense whiteness, as of lightning. Thea pulled aside one of the curtains. An arc-lamp spotlight, mounted upon a truck, was being played down Breitenbachplatz. The newspaper phrase *predawn raid* came immediately to mind as caption to the tableau beneath.

She opened the leftmost French door. Lang was standing beside her now. The oval of arc light halted on a section of the building frontage across the street. She gazed for a long while before she saw the man pressed to the building line.

"You!" said a voice, amplified horribly by loudspeaker.

Thea turned to Lang and said, "Do you see him?"

Then the man sprang away from the wall, leaving his shadow upon it. He broke north, sprinting up Breitenbachplatz. The spotlight moved jerkily, overshooting its target, backing up, overshooting once more.

"You were in a riot once," Thea said softly, recalling an anecdote he'd once related to her. She turned to face him. The light hit him from below, lending Expressionist menace to his strong features. Two anecdotes really. One when he was in the hospital. The other, on his way to make his first film.

Lang said, "Yes."

The spotlight caught up with the running man, stalled now. He was feinting to the left, to the right. A uniformed man—police or SA, it was hard to tell at this distance—advanced with deliberation. He was perhaps two meters in front of the running man.

"You," the loudspeaker repeated. "There is no escape."

Another spotlight truck pulled up from the direction of Potsdamer. Thea heard a deep metallic clunk as the second arc was fired up. It was trained almost immediately upon the two men, multiply shadowed, staring at one another against an unendurable whiteness. The running man, head bowed, was very still. They were coming up behind him.

Someone yelled, "Over here!"

The cornered man looked beyond the shoulder of his pursuer, as if acknowledging a comrade. The man in the uniform—it was SA, Thea could tell now—turned his head. In an instant the running man had gone around his blind side. The light on her husband's face was no longer melodramatic. Thea watched him regard the street. He was looking at the running man; but it seemed to her as if he were elsewhere, thinking of something which occurred a long time ago, or in a far place.

One arc swung wildly, its beam crossing the other once and again. Thea heard the barking of confused, contradictory orders.

The SA man had spun around but had not for some reason given chase. He remained as if pinned by the light in the spot where he had been deceived, casting a long dejected shadow up the steps of a Breitenbachplatz town house.

Thea watched a smile flicker briefly at the corner of her husband's mouth.

The brownshirt hung his head in front of him, as if waiting for something to fall. It was the posture the running man had assumed, just before making good his escape. At the shadows' edge Thea made out much scampering and could hear, more distantly now, the continued barking of commands. It was clear they'd caught neither the running man nor his accomplice, the one who'd yelled, "Over here!" She looked at Lang who continued staring at the street. "What?" she asked quietly.

Lang took a couple of steps backward, retreating into the living room without turning his head or averting his gaze. A tear was escaping the outside corner of his left eye. He inserted the monocle abruptly. Lang stood there, rubbing his shoulder beneath the crimson dressing gown. It was the site, Thea knew, of his war wounds. The tear seemed to be adhering to the lower rim of the monocle, which it did not overspill.

"I don't know why I make film," he said finally.

Thea wanted to put her arms around him. She knew it had been a long time since she was any solace to him. She wondered whether she had ever been able to comfort him; and decided that yes, at the beginning, and for some time after that, she had. It was a power whose loss had not been remarked upon at the time. The running man's face, indistinct in the arc lamp's glare, had not been unlike Sam's. Had it been Sam, caught in a last desperate attempt to get through to her? The more she thought the more she became certain that the running man's gait had not been anything like Sam's, not anything at all. Perhaps Sam had been the comrade, the confederate, the one who had shouted. She found herself recalling the number of her coat check ticket from the Scala, which was 154. Outside the voice—overamplified, clipped, distorted by loudspeaker horn and street acoustics—was saying, "It's all over."

She looked at Lang, still elsewhere. "All back to sleep," the voice went on. Lang sipped absently at his chocolate. She wondered what he would write in his diary tonight. And watched her husband add, to his chocolate, several teaspoons of sugar.

S E V E N

HE'D NOT BEEN SLEEPING WELL. SATURDAY night, after watching the *tableau policier* beneath his balcony, he sat in the red leather chair past dawn, beyond exhaustion. The script was finished, but the energies he had summoned for its completion stayed with him. (Sirens, klaxons, commands continued as well, more distantly, well into daybreak.) Lang wondered why he'd been so naive as to assume everything would be, at once, better. He'd written a page of *Fiaker* no different really than the ones which preceded it; except that it was the last page.

Sunday, the latest glorious installment of what Lang took to be a false spring, Lang wandered Tiergarten fixing his eyes on landscape, on people, until they were no longer illustrations of one or another shot in the scenario he'd just finished. When he returned to the apartment the deskman delivered a handwritten note from Dr. Goebbels. Goebbels would meet him Monday at Lang's club, the Explorers'. They would either lunch there or go to the ministry depending, the note said, "on the progress of redecoration." Lang spent Sunday night running *The Testatament of Doctor Mabuse* on the white ceiling above his sleepless bed. Toward four A.M. Lang was not certain whether he was remembering *Testament* or dreaming it.

Now, at the Explorers', Lang sat in the drawing room's best high-backed chair, commanding a view of the over-sized fireplace, bookcases twice his height, and the intricate carved doors. He was drinking armagnac before noon, alternating sips of the brandy with gulps of bitter Explorers' coffee. He could feel quite distinctly the ruin of his digestion. Best, he thought, to ease off on the coffee, which seemed to him quite acidic.

"Herr Lang desires?" said one of the waiters, looming now in front of him. Lang waved him away; and then, fearing he'd been brusque, fashioned a warm smile. The waiter, whose name was not coming to mind, smiled back. "If I should fall asleep," said Lang, "wake me by noon?"

"Certainly, Herr Lang."

As he reclined he felt his starched formal shirt to be constricting him about the belly. (He would have to work on his weight, quite soon.) The wing collar was chafing his neck but he did not want to unbutton it. He would simply tell Dr. Goebbels that *Testament* represented the hopes and fears of the German people; and that it was the duty of the filmmaker to depict his times. "I respect the audience," he would tell Goebbels, "which I believe to be moving toward better standards and higher truths on the screen as well in life." Lang wished for the reassuring presence of Nebenzal, who'd restrained him so diplomatically a week ago now in the UFA commissary. He did not want to lose his temper at Dr. G. . . . Best, Lang told himself, to recognize necessity.

He was seated quite near the fire, flickering highlights from which could be discerned on his face, and on the surface of the monocle. Yet he felt cold. He considered calling for a blanket, as one does on ship's deck. His mother had knitted him a blanket, while she'd been carrying him. It had been pink and blue, against each eventuality. Lang wondered now where the pink-and-blue blanket might be, and when he'd last seen it. It was, he decided, somewhere in Dahlem, probably toward the back of the cedar armoire.

Lang rubbed his shoulder, the old wound, which seemed to be feeling stiff of late; and then moved his hand to his upper lip, conscious of being one of the few Explorers without a mustache. He tried to recall whether Thea had mused what he'd look like with one, or whether she'd told him she was glad to have a clean-shaven man. He couldn't remember now. They had left the apartment this morning at the same time, he in the Lancia, she in the big car, he for the club, she for UFA. Apparently Correll was giving her a chance to direct. The project was *Elisabeth and the Fool*, one of those horrid weepy women's pictures whose script had been knocking around the studio for some time. As long as they don't assign her to *Fiaker*, he said to himself now, removing his monocle, passing it from hand to hand. He realized he was laughing aloud in a way which did not please him. Then, without any awareness of having been asleep, Lang felt a hand shaking him by the shoulder into wakefulness.

"Herr Lang?" It was the waiter whose name, it came to him now, was Heiner. Someone was standing to Heiner's left, someone whose face Lang—freshly wakened, without monocle—could not make out. Had Dr. Goebbels been watching him sleep? Lang felt his heart beat high in his chest. It beat twice in what seemed an impermissibly short interval.

Heiner said, "It's noon, sir." He moved to one side. The man he'd been obscuring was not Dr. Goebbels but rather another waiter, weighty silver coffeepot in hand.

"Thank you," Lang told Heiner; and to the waiter he added, "Yes, please." He drained the armagnac, handing the glass to Heiner. Circumstantial evidence. He wondered what kind of salary Thea could command as a director, on a scenario not her own. He inserted the monocle. The burnished wood bookshelves led down to a Kirghiz rug. In the far corner a rack of current newspapers, on sticks. The room lacked only a globe on which Kai Hoog—with coordinates boldly purloined, ingeniously deciphered—could plot the location of the diamond ship. Lang removed his monocle, finding the pattern of hearth flame more enticing without the clarity a corrective lens provides. Somewhere in the Club cellars was a bottle of Mouton-Rothschild '63 which he would probably never get to drink. The coffee was hotter now, but no less bitter.

Heiner walked toward him and said, "A telephone message sir. You are to be outside in three minutes."

"Thank you."

His striped trousers had gone baggy at the knees. Lang pulled down his shirt, which had ridden up, and tugged down the sleeves of his cutaway, fearful of flashing too much cuff. He stopped at the desk to pick up his homburg. It had not been sufficiently cold to require a topcoat. Donning the hat, centering it on his head, he recalled he'd intended to bring the *Fiaker* scenario with him, to drop it off at Nebenzal's Nero Films offices after lunch. But he'd left the script on the hallway table, next to the cut-glass vase. He'd have to return home at some point

173

and retrieve it. Outside it was immediately quite bright, and Lang shielded his eyes with one hand until they could stop down. It seemed to him that they adjusted to abrupt changes in brightness with far less alacrity than even six months ago. There were sirens off to his left. Finally he was able to gaze down Französichestrasse. He moved his hand downward, from forehead to upper lip. A mustache would make him look more Jewish. The sun was overhead now and cast a small puddle of shadow at his feet. The sirens were louder.

A pair of motorcycles came into view followed by a long car, then two more cycles. As they came toward him the motor noise grew louder until it was supreme over the sirens. Lang did not know why the sirens had been more audible from a distance.

The lead cycles pulled up to the curb ahead of him without stopping their engines.

Lang looked back toward the club. The Explorers' doorman was staring at him.

A brownshirt jumped off the near runningboard of the long open car—a Mercedes, Lang saw now—and held open the rear door. Lang entered, extended his hand. "How do you do."

"Very pleased to meet you," said Dr. Goebbels as Lang hitched his trousers and seated himself. They were moving at once. The cycles widened their distance and slowed slightly until the Mercedes was once more in their "pocket." He was shorter than Lang would have thought; and more handsome. He appeared several years Lang's junior.

"An honor," Lang said, moving his lips with some exaggeration. He could not hear his own voice over the engines, the sirens. Goebbels looked toward Lang and smiled. Goebbels was wearing a tan trench coat and a tie folded, rather than knotted, at the throat.

They slowed somewhat turning left onto Friedrichstrasse. "Already," said Goebbels, taking advantage of the diminished noise, "the swastika flies above public buildings, as the official flag!" He put a hand to Lang's shoulder, speaking directly into his ear. "What kind of car do you drive?"

"A roadster."

"What kind?" Goebbels repeated. They were taking a right on Kochstrasse. Lang put a hand to his hat, afraid it would blow away. He caught sight of six or seven spectators on the corner who had stopped to cheer on the procession. Lang found himself profoundly unused to this kind of applause.

"A Lancia," he said finally.

Goebbels said, "Fine, fine car."

Lang said, "As is this." It sounded quite stupid even as he said it, but he could think of no other response. Turning left on Wilhelmstrasse now there were quite a few pedestrians lined along the curb, acclaiming the motorcade. As they approached the Chancellory the crowd became two deep in spots. Then the cycles had halted, a hundred or so meters this side of the Chancellory, and on the opposite side of the street.

Goebbels stood and raised his hand in salute. A brownshirt opened the door on Goebbels's side. Lang followed him out. The four cyclists, dismounted now, escorted Lang and Goebbels to the building's tall wrought-iron gates, in the "pocket" formation. Through the gate, they walked down a leisurely gravel path. Goebbels was gesturing toward the grand brown stucco building. "Designed by

Schinkel. It was given to us a week ago. You will have to excuse the mess. It needs quite a bit of work to make it suitable."

"Schinkel," Lang heard himself repeat. An architect his father Anton would mention, as an exemplary builder of the civic edifice. He seemed to recall that Schinkel was Viennese, but was not sure.

A team of men was chipping away at the stucco with broad, flat chisels. Goebbels paused, threw his arms around the shoulders of two of them, returned to Lang. "My old and loyal SA bricklayers," he told Lang with some warmth.

At the double-height wooden door Goebbels turned to face the small crowd which had assembled at the gate as if for a premiere. Lang could discern one of them waving something which looked at this distance like an autograph book.

"The revolution," Goebbels said in a low formal tone, "proceeds throughout the Reich. We are living in a great and stupendous epoch. By the favor of Destiny I am allowed to take part in it."

Inside, several brownshirts were bent low, prying up wainscoting. Goebbels greeted two or three of them by name. The escort of cyclists remained outside; and alone now, they made their way up the dramatic central staircase. Goebbels walked, Lang was noticing, with a bit of a limp, and grasped occasionally at the banister. The staircase had marble treads which were strewn with old newspapers. The air was pungent with plaster dust.

"The old Leopoldpalast," said Goebbels.

Now they turned onto a seemingly endless corridor which led to the building's distant northern wing. Three brownshirts passed, walking with an exaggerated slowness.

They were carrying tall stacks of yellowed newsprint, which they held in front of them. One was bent backward, peering over the top of his freight. Lang turned to watch them reach the head of the staircase and let fly the papers. They were smiling at one another with a jocular athleticism. They were so young.

"I recall," said Lang, "an old joke, about the method used by one of my professors to grade examinations." He was hearing his own footsteps now, quite loudly.

"Yes," said Goebbels, grinning in comprehension. Goebbels was keeping the same side toward him. It was a vanity Lang was used to from Klein-Rogge but had not seen, as far as he could recall, in a nonprofessional. Lang's stomach, gone all heavy, was bothering him now. He wished he'd eaten something to absorb the Explorers' coffee.

Affixed to the door was a hand-lettered cardboard sign, tacked up slightly off-angle:

MINISTER OF STATE FOR PROPAGANDA AND
PUBLIC ENLIGHTENMENT

"They are preparing something engraved," Goebbels said, ushering his guest through.

There was a single oversized desk in a remote corner, and a meter-high globe, which would have done well in the Explorers' Club drawing room. Goebbels was pulling aside heavy draperies. The tall windows gave west onto Wilhelmstrasse. Dust motes swam in the bright, acutely angled window light. Again Lang sensed the brightness as painful. Goebbels, at the door, shouted, "Lucas! Hans!" Two SA men entered, and stood with their hands behind them.

"I cannot work in twilight," said Goebbels, pointing to the draperies. The brownshirts went at them with great ripping gestures which Lang found to his surprise quite satisfying to behold.

"We will have to do something," he said, standing close to Lang, "about the afternoon light, but these draperies will not do, will not do at all." Goebbels went around to the far side of the immense desk. Their work completed, the SA men departed, closing the door with some delicacy behind them. Much dust had been raised, which seemed to float upward, like steam, from the puddled draperies.

"Herr Lang," Goebbels began, voice harsher now, more metallic. Indeed, the entire room tone had changed. "The Leader and I many years ago were traveling, in the organization of our party. One night, in a small town in the northern part of our land, we took brief respite from the work of revolution and went to see a film. The film was your *Metropolis*. We were both profoundly moved. The Leader was particularly attentive to the reaction of the audience, which was enthusiastic." Lang waited for him to go on, but he did not. Finally Lang took a wooden chair from the doorway, pulled it to a spot just this side of the desk. Goebbels sat in shadow. The bare windows were admitting a harsh March sunlight, which did not quite reach him. Lang found his eyes did not have the dynamic range to accommodate the entire room at once.

"Thank you," Lang said.

He sat down. The chair had no side arms. He crossed his hands in front of him, not worrying about the drape of the gray formal coat. It was like school. Goebbels was going to make him sit, and wait, for the lecture about

Testament. He had been a bad boy, had gone and made a bad movie. The moral of the speech would come last. *With every privilege comes a responsibility.* It was always the same moral. "I'm gratified," Lang said now, hearing his words come back at him, no curtains now to muffle the hard, echoic expanse of glass. Lang heard traffic sounds from outside; and the brownshirt hammers, clanging sharp and random. There was a clock, outside the window, some blocks away, whose face was legible.

"I want to talk," said Goebbels in half shadow, "about the tasks of today's filmmaker."

Lang said, "Yes."

Goebbels shot his left cuff, consulting a wristwatch. "Less that a month ago I saw the first of the films we had commissioned. It was of a speech made by the Leader at the Sportpalast. Perhaps you were there. In any case, I found the film of suitable quality to use as propaganda toward the Day of an Awakening Nation. The film's good effect lies principally in uniformity of presentation, and in the good synchronization. In every town in which the Leader is unable to speak, it must be shown." Lang watched the crosshatched parallelograms of window light advance toward him across the dusty parquet floor. It was an exercise in discipline, Lang thought, akin to watching the minute hand of an outsized municipal clock. Within moments direct sunlight would be touching his shoe. Soon after he would be in the illuminated center of one of the parallelograms, circumscribed by muntin- and sash-shadow, as if snared within a web of fate.

"Every one of these meetings," Goebbels went on, "draws an entire province into its magic circle. It has been my task to enable listeners over the Radio to enter heart and soul into the spirit of these meetings. In the future Film will overtake Radio in its ability to perform this task. After the Leader and I saw *Metropolis* he turned to me and said, 'This is the man who will depict the creation of the new German nation. This is the man who will make the National Socialist film! ' A historic task, and one which not just anyone could assume." He pushed a cigarette box across the desk. It slid to a stop within Lang's reach. "I feel somewhat nervous," Goebbels said as Lang took a cigarette of indeterminate brand, "when I consider that I am only just over thirty-five, and burdened with such heavy responsibility."

"You are young," Lang heard himself say.

"Older than yourself when you made *Nibelungen*," said Goebbels. "It remains one of my personal quartet of most favored films."

Lang lit the cigarette with a kitchen match from his trouser pocket. It was of Turkish blend, somewhat oval. He found it mild, fragrant, altogether satisfying, though in a different way from his habitual Boyards.

"But I talk too much of film as documentation, I see, and not sufficiently of film as art," said Goebbels, leaning into Lang's exhalation. "Art is the noblest activity of the human soul and imagination. It is feeling that has become form. What the artist harbors in his heart he brings to expression in art." He withdrew from his breast pocket a white bristol card, covered both sides with fine jottings. He consulted it, went on. "Heightened feelings postulate heightened modes of expression. What the masses often only have as a dark and gloomy yearning, the artist expresses in Word, Music, Stone, or Marble." His voice became sonorous, exquisitely modulated. Lang jerked his head, realizing he'd been momentarily asleep. Goebbels, consulting his notes once more, appeared not to have noticed.

"Art has always exalted and impressed people. The artist brings them out of the dark humdrum of everyday existence into a better world. Indeed, whole areas of a new cultural and historical evolution have become enlightened and immortalized through it.

"Therefore, artists as divinely inspired interpreters of the deepest secrets of human life have always stood in the company of the Great in all other areas as well—"

A salient of window light had reached Lang's foot. He could go back home, pick up the *Fiaker* manuscript, perhaps even change to less formal attire, carry out the day's errands. He'd been able to visualize them perfectly, in the Explorers'; but now his itinerary was fading. He looked out to the clock. If he left now, or within the next five minutes, he could reach the bank before closing, withdraw his money.

"—It was always the noblest rule of the true blossom time of human culture and history for 'the Singer to walk with the King.' "

Lang found himself looking at the expanse of white wall above Goebbels's head. He thought of the pink-and-blue blanket, certain now that it was toward the rear of the top drawer in the cedar armoire, nestling among other comforting mementos of Viennese childhood. Lang was at once uncertain whether he wanted Nebenzal to read *Fiaker*; whether, in fact, he wanted anyone to read it.

"The Leader and I would like you to join us," Goebbels was saying, indicating with hand movements that he was drawing to a close, "in helping to express, indeed to forge, the wonderful steely romanticism of our times."

Lang was pleased that Goebbels had mentioned the *Nibelungen* epic, rather than *Metropolis*. *Metropolis* the obvious choice, the one the Leader had mentioned, the one which seemed to please the crowds no end. In a strange way he didn't think of it as his film at all.

"Just out of curiosity, the other three?" Lang said finally.

Goebbels was looking at him.

"In your quartet of favorite films," Lang added.

Goebbels snapped the bristol card to its other side. "*Anna Karenina*, I should think. *Potemkin*. And *The Rebel*, which impressed me more than any film I have seen this year, and which I think may prove sufficiently strong to withstand the test of time." Goebbels adjusted his folded-over tie. Lang's treasured voile shirt had a collar quite similar to the one Goebbels was wearing now.

" 'The singer to walk with the King,' " said Goebbels for a second time, indicating quotation marks with his voice.

Lang extinguished the Turkish cigarette on a cut-glass ashtray, which held down some papers on the near corner of the desk. He had been brought here that Goebbels might inquire whether he'd be willing to become the state's official filmmaker. The butt continued to smolder. Apparently, he'd put the cigarette out badly. Lang mashed it with his thumb.

Goebbels was saying, "Do you need some time?"

Lang shut his eyes briefly and saw, in that interior theater, the *Fiaker* manuscript, lying still and diagonal on the hall table; his diary book, the cap of the special pen just touching its corner; and the childhood blanket, folded just so, the way he'd last seen it, before shutting the cedar drawer. Lang opened his eyes and said quietly, "My mother."

He made himself look at Goebbels.

"My mother, Paula Schlesinger, was Jewish," said Lang after a while. His forehead and upper lip were quite wet now. A wave as of relief had broken over him. Thoughts which had come into his head of the past few weeks, of obscure origin, became at once clear now that he'd said it.

"Your war service," said Goebbels.

Lang looked toward the floor. He was now totally within the frame of shadowy crossbars, none of which at this moment quite touched him. He was bathed in direct sunlight.

"In the future we shall have those fortunate to be born National Socialists. Until that day we shall all of us be, in one sense or another, converts." Goebbels reached for the stack of papers held down by the cut-glass ashtray. Several of them bore the UFA letterhead and appeared to be handouts from the studio's publicity department. "It says that you were arrested by the Paris police at the commencement of hostilities, managed to evade them, catching the last train to Vienna. Is this so?"

Lang said, "Yes," and lit one of his own cigarettes. It was more or less true. He'd been arrested, actually, not in Paris, but at the Belgian border.

"Served at the front with the Imperial Austrian Army. Wounded three times. Decorations."

"Yes," Lang said again.

A clatter of hammers, which Goebbels waited out. "Your service bespeaks a great patriotism, and a will of no small strength. In this light any questions of, say, ancestry can easily be overlooked."

183

Lang had told Goebbels about his mother, and it had not been enough. His shirt was damp with the sweat of relief which now seemed to him wholly inappropriate, but which clung to him when he moved his arms to light the cigarette.

Lang listened to the sounds of the SA men striking, he mused uncharitably, the old set. Goebbels picked up the telephone which he realized had not rung since they'd been in the room. Goebbels dialed a number and said without preface, "How are we doing for Potsdam? *This* Wednesday. If you have any particular needs for transportation or lodging, spend what's necessary of course. Yes. I expect you here tomorrow. Ten A.M.? Very well. Until then." Lang had been gazing at the clock outside the window. Even if he were to leave right now, he'd not make the bank by two-thirty closing.

"The opening of the new Reich," Geobbels explained. "We're going to broadcast it throughout the nation, by Radio."

Lang rubbed his shoulder.

"I have called a gathering of film producers, at the Kaiserhof, for the evening of the twenty-eighth. I want to set forth a new program for the cinema. We've been given the impression that all invited are honestly willing to cooperate. The scheduling of this event so soon after my assumption of leadership of this ministry shall serve as public notice of the importance of the film medium to our nation. Film can only be reestablished on a healthy basis if German nationality is remembered in the industry, and the German nature portrayed by it. The gathering will be informal. We would like you to chair it, to establish from the beginning the esteem in which you are held by us, and the power which you can expect to command, in Germany's behalf."

Lang worked the phrasing out in his head, then said, "You must give me some time in which to think this over. I have always thought of myself, you must understand, as a filmmaker rather than an administrator. Much of what you have said is new to me. Can you allow me twenty-four hours, to spend in thought and in consultation with my wife, before reaching a decision?"

Goebbels smiled and said, "Most certainly."

Lang stood up.

"Please tell your wife," Goebbels said, "how much I admire her collection of stories, *The War and the Women*. It had a great influence upon me, upon all writers of our generation. 'Beloved Fatherland' in particular. You will remember to tell her?"

Lang said, "She will be quite pleased."

Goebbels stood. He said, "You can reach me here tomorrow morning. After that I will be fairly preoccupied by Potsdam."

Then Goebbels walked around the desk, still keeping his best profile toward Lang. Both men were out of shadow now. They shook hands. Goebbels said, "I regret that we did not have the opportunity to meet sooner."

"Yes."

He asked Lang, "Will you have any trouble finding your way out?"

"No."

"Forgive me for not escorting you."

In the corridor now, Lang was closing the door behind him. It was a wonder that Goebbels could place *The Rebel* in his pantheon. He had seen it, at an UFA screening; and it had been a piece of shit. Lang realized the extent to which his shirt, and underclothes, were wet with sweat. If he did not wash soon, he would begin to stink, like his old friend Brecht.

A brownshirt, mostly hidden behind a tall stack of magazines, approached from the opposite end of the corridor. He tossed his cargo down the staircase, made an abrupt about-face toward the corridor's distant end.

One of the side doors opened, flinging a diagonal of light across the marble floor. Lang was about to reach its edge when the door closed, sweeping the light up with it.

Now Lang found himself at the head of the staircase He would take a taxi home, change, book a reservation on the sleeper to Paris under an assumed name. His passport, if he recalled correctly, was in good order

Lang consulted his pocket watch. Two-thirty. The bank had just closed. Perhaps he could give Nebenzal power of attorney, have his funds wired to Paris. More probably Thea would get the house in Dahlem, the Breitenbachplatz apartment, the money. It didn't matter much in any case.

He wondered whether he had time to drive out to Dahlem, take some of his pre-Columbiana. Best not to think about it. He could take the bird, from the mantelpiece, which he could fit into a suitcase, or plausibly stuff in an overcoat pocket.

Lang descended the wide marble staircase, its risers and treads—concave from long use—littered with newsprint, and with the rubble of deconstruction work. He wondered now whether he might find Thea at home. He would have to call Nebenzal, to find out if the producer had gotten hold of the *Testament* negative. Lang would take it with him. If not, surely it would not be impossible to find some way of getting the thing shipped on.

He reached the bottom of the staircase, walked directly toward the outside doors. He would book the sleeper under the name of von Wenk, the hapless prosecutor. A small inside joke, Lang thought, which he could afford just now. He reinserted the monocle. The doors began to open outward as if the guards, or the outside, had somehow been aware of his approach. Lang braced himself for the onslaught of sunlight.

The light was flooding the widening slit. Lang walked into it. Outside, he realized he'd left his hat in Goebbels's office. Goebbels hadn't mentioned *Testament*, not once. Either he'd never intended to, or he'd forgotten. There was really no point in speculating.

Lang did not have much time but decided to walk for a while before hailing the cab. He had no problem at the gate, where the small crowd displayed no interest in the hatless departing man. Half a block down Lang found himself amazed that Goebbels had listened *Potemkin* among his favorite films. He would have to write Eisenstein, whom he recalled now with some affection. The Russian had passed through Berlin perhaps four years ago. Eisenstein had told Lang again and again how much *Doctor Mabuse, The Gambler* meant to him, how he'd learned to edit by taking apart *Mabuse* and reassembling it in various ways. Later, well into a bottle of chilled, sentimental vodka, they discovered their fathers were both municipal architects; and that like himself, Sergei had been strongly urged to take up that profession.

E I G H T

THEY WERE ABOUT TO DETOUR THE HANGAR-
like soundstage, constructed of coarse-grained cement,
which lay between them and the parking lot. Then a loud
annoying buzzer sounded three times, and the red light
above the sound stage door went out. Correll said, "We
may as well go through." He took her arm just above the
elbow. It was an innocent gesture, really, but one with
which Thea was not at all comfortable. She clutched her
handbag closer to her side. It rested nicely there, just
above the hip.

At the far end of the sound stage eight or ten arc
lamps, in a circle, aimed downward from high cross-
braced stanchions. The arc rods gave off a fair bit of
smoke, and the air was amiably charged with ozone. The
arcs gave out a strong and relentless illumination: the
interior of the circle was unwatchably bright. They walked
toward it. In Thea's handbag was a night letter which the
deskman had handed her as she and Lang had quit the
apartment this morning. She'd not yet opened it.

The set was of a carnival. At its center was a large
vertically mounted wheel, equipped with manacles and
balloons about its circumference. The manacles were un-
done at the moment; and an actress, whose face was
familiar to her, was just now departing the circle of light.

She was wearing a sequined leotard and had a towel about her shoulders. Thea looked downward, evading glare. She was within a meter of the camera before she recognized the man seated behind it. He was Fritz Arno Wagner, who had shot many of the films which Thea had written, and her husband directed. She'd not seen him since the night Lang had pressed his color-coded buttons, and toppled the chemical factory. Flames licking the night sky.

An assistant was removing the film magazine from the camera and replacing it with a new one.

Correll let go her arm and said, "Are you ready for all this?" in a soft voice.

"Oh absolutely." Thea switched her bag, with its tantalizing cargo, to the other side. The spangled woman was now pacing before the large five-spoked wheel. A man Thea took to be the director was fussily smoothing the towel around her shoulder.

Wagner looked up and Thea said, "Hello, Fritz Arno." Wagner smiled. Correll said, "I would like to present UFA's newest director." They looked away toward the manacles, the balloons. The camera assistant, his chore accomplished, walked rapidly away from the illuminated zone. He seemed to be able to avoid the cables without looking down. The director trotted over and said, "Are you ready?" Wagner nodded. "She wants to know," the director went on, "why you can't just spin the camera."

"A little late for that now," said Wagner.

Correll put his mouth to Wagner's ear and said, "Would you have any problems—"

"Spin the camera?" the director repeated, with an unpleasant inflection.

"Tell her," Wagner said to the director, "we're in on her tight, like this." He indicated chin-to-forehead with rigid parallel hands.

"—working for a woman?"

The director trotted back toward the carnival.

"Not this one," said Wagner, giving Thea a broad wink. He'd photographed Thea's film for Murnau, *Burning Soil*, as well as *Nosferatu*, the one about the vampire. She had known him for well over a decade. Since *Destiny* at least. Around the time she'd taken up with Lang.

Correll was saying, "That is what I wanted to hear." He took Thea's arm once more. The night letter in her handbag bore the letters PTT at the end of the jumble preceding her address, leading Thea to believe it had originated somewhere in France, perhaps Paris.

Wagner put his eye to the side of the camera, adjusting something with his right hand. "They are strapping that actress to a wheel," he told her, "which they intend to spin rapidly. That's before they start throwing the knives. She doesn't want to do it. I don't know why. Are you sure, Thea dear, this is the way you wish to make your living?"

"A little late for that now," said Thea finally. Correll was leading her away toward the light- and soundproof double doors.

"Congratulations, by the way," Wagner called after her.

Someone said, "Quiet please!"

As they reached the door Thea heard the director say, "Camera?"

Wagner said, "Camera." Thea did not turn around.

"Sound?"

"Speed."

The director said, "And action."

She paused momentarily at the first door, bracing herself against the shotlike sound of bursting balloons; but the report didn't come, and she allowed Correll to usher her through. She supposed had anything gone hideously wrong, she would have heard the scream.

Over lunch she and Correll had discussed *Elisabeth and the Fool*, which he wanted her to rewrite and to direct. Within a week she'd have a starting date, late spring, early summer. There seemed to be only a small reluctance on his part to meet her salary. They wanted an exclusive option on her services for five years, which Thea found excessive; but there was time to negotiate that later. Outside, she found the strap of her left shoe had somehow gotten twisted. Thea leaned up against the rough cement wall as she ran a finger beneath the strap. Straightening up she saw the bulky black Mercedes toward the middle of the parking lot. It was the car their driver Erich customarily piloted; but he'd gotten sick, or so he said, two weeks ago, and had not been heard from since. This morning her husband had appropriated the Lancia, without a word.

"We'll speak," she was telling Correll. She resented driving the Mercedes, which was simply too large to handle with any ease.

"Yes," he replied bending low over her hand, hovering there for quite some time. Thea decided she would wait until she got home before allowing herself to read the wire. She noticed that Correll had a well-defined bald spot, the size of a large coin, at the top of his head.

"Good-bye," she said finally. For a short moment there was an expression on his face which she had seen before, on Lang, and on Sam, on every man, really, she'd ever known. Then he turned, retracing his steps toward the double doors which led to the interior of the stage, fragrant with ozone. The spot at the crown of his head was not unlike a monk's tonsure. Opening the car door Thea found the palm of her hand marked with red indentations where she'd leaned up against the cement moments before. Or had it been concrete? She seemed to recall from somewhere that concrete had rocks in it, cement not. It was very bright outside, the sky deep blue and cloudless save the occasional wispy cirrus. Thea wondered how they would cool the windowless sound stage when it got to be summer.

She hoped that Lang had managed to convince them to lift the ban on *Testament*. He would be far more human with the film in release. She hoped as well that he did not lose his temper, or behave badly, with Dr. Goebbels, in ways which would have unfortunate repercussions for his career, or for hers.

Thea backed out of the lot, driving slowly past the black tower, and the newer Bauhaus structure, down the graveled access road.

The renovation of the Dahlem house would be done, the contractor had told her, within the week. Then she could ransom the dogs from the kennel, have a place of her own once more. Now that she knew when she would be able to live separately from him, Thea found much of her rancor toward Lang was evaporating. Perhaps her sweeter feelings, held down for so long, could rise now to the surface. She was discovering she wished him well, for the first time really since the holidays.

The Mercedes veered sharply south, toward Berlin proper.

Thea turned the pneumatic windshield wipers on, and off; and then laughed, because it was not raining and the windshield was quite dry. She took her hand from the control knob and brought it to her face, rubbing her eyes, which for some reason were stinging quite badly now.

Stopping for a railroad crossing she looked to the side, noticing the inevitable bicyclist in knickers and cloth cap. A freight train lumbered past, car by car, giving out low rhythmic clatter. Then it was gone. The pike before her bore thick black-and-yellow stripes, on the bias. As it lifted the bicyclist yelled something to her; and then turned sharply left, pedaling off toward the far horizon, where the rails converged. If she'd not been mistaken he'd said, "Berlin stays red!" or something close to it. It made no sense. She was alongside the Sportpalast garden and, crossing Goerdelerdamm with the light, was once more within city limits. Her cheeks were wet and she supposed she must have been crying, before, when she'd turned the wipers on. "That was a funny thing to do," she said aloud now. Then she was on Hüttenstrasse. The traffic had become quite thick. A column of cyclists streamed by. The factories must be letting out.

Thea patted the seat beside her until she felt the clasp of her handbag. She could pull over now, she knew, and read the night letter; but upon reflection it seemed better to wait until she was home. She could stop by the Zuntz to see if Sam were there or if he'd left any message for her. It wasn't really out of the way. She could pull up to the curb, speak to the barman, and be on her way again in a matter of seconds.

The sun, behind her now, turned windows gold, and brickwork a deep, Aztec red, against darkening eastern sky. It was her favorite time of day. A small blue sportscar swerved in front of the Mercedes, cutting her off, and causing her to curse audibly.

Now the Gedächtniskirche was on her left. Thea slowed, turned her head, but did not see the Zuntz. There was an unfamiliar gate of iron pantograph gridwork, padlocked top and bottom. Pulling to the curb she could see enough of the cursive gold Z to remove any doubt. She had never known the Zuntz to be closed before midnight. Thea cut the engine and busied herself with the Countess Told holder. The cigarette was for some reason too fat and had to be twisted into place. The Forget-Me-Not, she remembered, had been "closed by the police," whatever that meant; 31 Linkstrasse was a dirt lot; and now the Zuntz was inexplicably shuttered. It was as if one of Friedrich's horrid little men, before the Pigeon Board, were revising the map of Berlin, obliterating Sam's footsteps behind him. Now making fine crosshatches in India ink over the Zuntz storefront. Then, mounting his dark-wood stepladder with a muttered oath, brushing opaque white fluid over a half-block stretch of Linkstrasse. Deleting from the cityscape any site which might hold out, for the American, some solace.

Thea lowered the window, realizing only now how smoky the car's interior had become. She gazed down the street toward the church, toward the spot where Sam had stood with his pathetic baby camera, documenting the Circus Bustello, the true circus of Mexico. Now she saw nothing but a clot of pedestrians, shoppers laden with parcels, a few small children grabbing wildly at their mothers' hems. She regarded the street for quite a while, until the children had passed. None of them had the hair, the face, of the one who'd smiled so memorably at Nüburgring. After *Elisabeth* they'd surely let her try something of her own. It would be wonderful if they would release sufficient funds for her to mount her Arabian scenario properly. A strong love story at its center, she saw now, would let her have immense fun around the edges, with detail, and with the characterizations of the supporting players. Thea found herself tapping the steering column in delighted contemplation of just what she could do, two films from now. Then she was on Breitenbachplatz.

A man in a leather overcoat, carrying a Gladstone bag and a bulging satchel in either hand, was stepping to the curb in front of Thea's building. The gateman, beside him now, was whistling for a cab. She couldn't be sure for a moment whether it was her husband. A cab pulled to a stop between them. Something large, of stone, protruded from the side pocket of his belted leather overcoat. The way he ducked his head to enter the cab made Thea sure beyond doubt she was watching Lang.

Thea worked her horn but the cab pulled off and she could not manage, with the cars in front of her and to her left, to make a U-turn. She would have to wait for the corner.

She reached it just as the light went red.

The way Lang had stood there, bag in each hand, just before ducking into the cab, persisted in her vision as she regarded the spotlight. Her stomach seemed abruptly to fall downward, away from her. She felt, unalterably, *too late*. It was something like the feeling she'd had last night, in the streets of the working-class district; but now it was just twilight and the feeling was far worse. As if something terrible had happened while she'd not been paying attention, and all her efforts from here on futile, useless, doomed to failure. The light turned green. Hers was the only car not advancing. (She recalled a car pausing before a green light: the way we learn of the death of Doctor Kamm, in *Testament*.) Then the rest of the traffic passed around her and she executed a U-turn.

She passed by the entrance to her apartment and drove without pause down Breitenbachplatz. She thought she could see the taxi farther down.

She came to a halt at the corner. The light had turned red and it would have been suicidal, in this cross traffic, to have attempted to run it.

A blue double-decker municipal bus passed in front of her, left to right. A child in a sailor cap was holding a helium balloon, the string around his wrist. The balloon was of a color identical to that of the bus. Then the bus was gone. Thea heard a sharp report, and wondered momentarily whether she were hearing the burst of the blue balloon. The sound, she decided, was far too loud. More, really, like an engine's backfire. She recalled having listened for, and not heard, the popping of balloons, earlier today, at UFA.

The light before her remained red for a longer time than she would have felt possible. By the time it went green Thea had already decided to pull the car to the curb and park it.

She walked carefully back to the apartment, working hard now to maintain good posture. Neither the man at the gate nor the man behind the desk had anything to say to her. The stairwell odor was oppressively familiar. There was a crack of light beneath the door to her apartment.

Thea extracted her key chain from the handbag. She looked at her keys until she could recall which was the proper one. She took the proper one and fitted it in the lock.

On the foyer table, next to the cut-glass vase, were two keys bound with a short, clumsily knotted length of string. She recognized the string, with its blue-and-white twist, as from the patisserie. Looking closer she saw the Lancia emblem on the shank of the topmost key. Then she saw the piece of paper, irregularly torn, beneath the vase.

She slid the paper toward her and could make out the writing, which was her husband's:

CAR AROUND THE CORNER FROM EXPLORERS' CLUB

Taking the piece of paper with her Thea sat down before the hearth. It would be nice to have a fire. She contemplated fixing the kindling, throwing logs on the andiron. It seemed far too much to do right now.

The mantel was strangely smooth. It hit her that the pre-Columbian bird, Lang's favored object, was gone from its perch on the mantel. She had never seen the mantel without it before.

She recalled the stony protrusion she'd seen, stuck out at an odd angle from the pocket of her husband's leather coat just before the taxi had intervened, right to left.

After a while she slid off her coat and toyed idly with

the patent surface of her handbag. Then she reached into the bag, extracting the night letter.

DARLING THEA COMMA DEPARTURE IN NEW
AFFECTION AND NEW NOISE STOP ALL MY LOVE
SIGNED MARK HULL

Mark Hull was the detective in the American pulp magazine whose saga Sam had persisted in relating to her in the Zuntz, the last time they had seen each other. The message would have to be a quotation. Perhaps later she would look through her editions of Rimbaud, of Lautréamont, and track it down.

Sam was safe in Paris. The fear, which she had been holding back from thinking in so many words, was that he'd been arrested somewhere last night. But last night he was in Paris. It was a piece of news which an hour ago would have afforded her a great relief, but which now seemed beside the point.

It was perceptibly darker outside. She directed her eyes toward the window, watching the frontage of the building across the street gradually become supplanted by the reflection of her own face.

Closing her eyes Thea saw a blue-white arc light, bigger and more powerful than any she'd ever seen, aimed upward from the darkness of central Tiergarten. It projected a broad focused cone of unutterable brightness. Then a small flock of pigeons flew into that cone, throwing up spears of darkness which weaved and danced above them as they passed through it. Thea considered the fluttering black shafts cast up by the pigeons, stunned and unknowing, momentarily distracted on their way back to

Alex. (The running man must have been quite fast, quite evasive, to have caused all those pigeons to be released, nearly simultaneously. *Perhaps*, it occurred to her now, *there was more than one running man*.) Upthrust light, dark upward shadows: an image Thea told her self to save, for the film she was already thinking of as *Secret Arabia*.

Had she opened the wire in the morning she would have known not to stop at the Zuntz. Would she have been able to see her husband before his departure? Might have changed all. But there was really no way, she told herself finally, she could have known. She opened her eyes. Then at once Thea felt as if she understood what had happened. She watched her double, in the living room just beyond the window, draw herself up to full height.

The door to the Pullman compartment was not closing fully. Lang saw that a small copper coin had gotten wedged against the jamb rail. He pocketed the coin—a Belgian ten-franc piece—for luck, and pushed the door shut. He had, in fact, booked the compartment in the name of von Wenk. By the time he would have to produce his passport, at the border, it would no longer matter that the name did not correspond.

He patted his breast pocket just to make sure he'd not forgotten his passport. Then extracted it, riffling his thumb along the edge. He'd last taken this train in April of 1932 with Nebenzal and Peter Lorre, for the Paris premiere of *M*. They'd given him a year-long visa which, he reassured himself now, had not quite expired. (There were also four months left, he saw now, on an old visa for England, which might or might not be useful.) Lang regarded the photo, affixed with two hollow tin rivets. It was not a bad likeness as these things go, and depicted a man thinner than he knew himself to be now. Friedrich Christian Anton Lang. With the left hand Lang parted the pocket from the lining, and with his right dropped the passport home.

Afraid that he might have been followed from the Ministry, Lang had timed his arrival at the platform for five-twenty-nine, a bare minute before scheduled departure. (It seemed somehow that this would give Goebbels less time to make up his mind that Lang should be detained.) Now it was, by his pocket watch, five-thirty-four. He sensed no movement. Pulling back the edge of the cloth shade Lang put his eye to the window. The platform remained motionless. There did not seem to be any sense of havoc among the few dozen milling trackside extras. Panning the crowd scene to feature individual faces he saw neither elegant Wieland nor ham-fisted Bott. Lang gave some attention to the train on the platform opposite, then patted the window shade back into place. Reaching into the outside pocket of the leather satchel he extracted the pearl-handled straight razor.

Lang heard the harsh escaping steam of a train whistle, twice; but he was not sufficiently versed in railway code to know what that might signify. He tested the edge of the blade against the side of his thumb—the same light riffling motion he'd used, moments before, with the passport. Taking to his knees, Lang knelt beneath the washstand. He considered the razor. Then, in one deliberated stroke, he slashed through the carpet. The adhesive which held the carpet to its backing gave easily. Lang slipped a wad of bills from his outside jacket pocket into the slit. He

200

had twenty-seven thousand marks—far more than you were allowed to take with you, to another country.

Returning to his seat he tried to convince himself that the bulge was not apparent if you were not looking for it. The slit was largely concealed by the shadow line cast by the basin's edge. It was not a bad job actually, not at all.

He brought his fingers to his nose. They smelled sweet, tropical. Lang recalled the carpet glue at UFA. He smiled, pleased he'd made the association so efficiently.

The train whistle gave a solitary shriek, much longer this time, and of higher pitch. Lang was in the third car from the rear of the train, and there were perhaps a dozen more cars in front.

Back at Breitenbachplatz, after his session with Goebbels, Lang had removed the cutaway, the stiff collar. Then, bare-chested, packed a few clothes and some valuables. As he had walked from bedroom to living room Lang envisaged a scene where the fugitive, having told his butler to pack a weekend case, surreptitiously slips his stud box and some items of jewelry beneath a folded pair of trousers while the butler's attention is diverted. If filmed correctly, Lang thought, the audience will know at once that the man is leaving for good. He had paused, both hands on the suitcase lid, to work it out shot for shot.

Lang left Thea a note with the keys to the Lancia. Then he'd made himself sit, for half an hour, so as not to arrive at Zoo Station prematurely. He busied himself on the phone, leaving a message for Nebenzal about the necessity of getting the *Testament* negative back from UFA. Then he'd called Lily, but she was not at home, and after twenty rings Lang replaced the receiver. It was silly to think she would have to be at home. He'd send her a letter from Paris inviting her to visit, to spend some time. The accusations and suspicions, nearly thirteen years old now, would not have to follow. There was really no limit to what he could do, in Paris.

Then there were ten minutes left before the time he had said he'd allow himself to quit the apartment. It occurred to him that Thea might return at any moment. When it was time—a little after, really—Lang had walked past the desk, and had Josef hail him a cab.

Now there was an abrupt pneumatic jerk as if the train were starting up. It did not seem to be followed by any appreciable motion. Lang raised the shade, to see if the platform were sliding backward; but it was not. He decided to leave the shade up. It was dark in the Pullman compartment and an open shade, he felt now, would draw less attention than a closed one. (The window was, at any rate, glazed with dust.) Lang's molar began to throb, small twinges of pain, nothing intolerable. He would have to find a new dentist.

Lang unfastened once more the thick leather straps of his Gladstone. He found the stud box, a heavy gold cigarette case, and a roll of adhesive tape, which he stuffed into both trouser pockets. Looking into the bag he realized he'd not taken the script of *Fiaker*. He could recall moving it from the foyer table to his bed. That was his last clear image of the thing, one corner enfolded by the comforting chenille spread. Tomorrow from Paris he could wire Thea, ask her to send it on. But it didn't seem really to matter now.

Lang carefully pulled back the door, peering both ways down the corridor, as anyone might. He turned right. The corridor smelled of damp wool, cleaning fluid, coal exhaust. It was an ambient fragrance vaguely similar to that of the stairwell at Breitenbachplatz, but only vaguely. The odor was comforting to him. He thought suddenly of the objects, and paintings, in Breitenbachplatz and Dahlem, whose possession he'd now given up. One by one images of the objects came up on him, the only way now he'd ever see them.

The WC was at the end of the corridor. Inside Lang latched the door. Then, standing on the closed toilet lid, he fastened the stud box and the cigarette case to the inside of the overhead tank with long strips of adhesive tape. He tore the tape from the roll with some difficulty, using his teeth. It was the work of a minute and a half to secure the objects in their cache; and Lang felt himself profoundly satisfied. In Paris, or in Hollywood, when the time came to make the film about the fugitive, he'd include this scene. Perhaps he might let on, to his intimates, that it was closer to the truth than they'd ever know.

At once the stench of disinfectant in the small unventilated WC was too much to bear, and Lang reentered the corridor. He recalled the photo of himself and Lubitsch at the edge of the sunlit swimming pool, from his two-week stay in Hollywood. He had picked up some English in the States, had tried, back in Berlin, not to lose it. UFA had hired two kids, the American Mankiewicz and the Englishman Hitchcock, to translate the *Metropolis* title cards. Lang would dine with them at the commissary, insisting they not use German in front of him. Hitchcock was directing several films a year now, mostly from London; and Joe Mankiewicz wrote screenplays in Los Angeles. The last he'd heard from him, four years ago now,

Mankiewicz had just done an adaptation of *The Mysterious Doctor Fu-Manchu.*

Now Lang was at the end of the Pullman car, and found himself sliding back the door to the car behind. It was the dining car, dark now, unoccupied, glasses upside down on starched white tablecloths. To his left Lang saw a small rectangular box of varnished wood, used for refund slips. There was a small gap between it and the wall of the car. Lang reached into his breast pocket and extracted that portion of his cash he'd not hid beneath the carpet. (There were five hundred marks in all, enough for perhaps a week.) He took the sheaf, folded it in thirds lengthwise, slid it behind the refund box. The money was not visible, as far as he could ascertain, from any angle, save directly above. He felt the urge to laugh. Then he could no longer contain himself and a succession of wild, hideous grins erupted across his face. Finally he was able to swallow. It was like school, really, when the boy next to you passed you a note, reminding you how much trouble you'd get into, if you laughed.

He stepped across the gap between the diner and the Pullman on tiptoe, in a burlesque of secrecy. Then he slid the Pullman door shut behind him.

A man was approaching, about halfway down the long Pullman corridor now. He wore a wide-brimmed hat. The overhead illumination kept his face in shadow, save the brief instants when he was just between two bulbs. He seemed quite young, more a teenager pretending to be an adult than a full-fare passenger in his own right.

"Herr Lang?" he said hesitantly.

Lang said nothing.

"I'm Andreas Freund." He extended his hand. "Lotte's fiancé. She's Herr Kosterlitz's secretary?"

Lang shook his hand.

The young man went on, "I'm her fiancé. We met the night of the fire."

"Yes," said Lang, patting the younger man on the shoulder as he walked, around him, toward the compartment. There was no evidence he could think of that he was not just another man with two or three days' business in Paris. (There was, it hit him, the pre-Columbian figure, still in his overcoat pocket; but he could say he was taking it to Paris to get it appraised or some such. He'd tell them to call Professor Umlauff, at the Ethnography Museum, if there were any question.)

Lang wondered now what Freund had meant by "the night of the fire." Lang worked the door to his compartment. He supposed he had been brusque with the young man. Putting a hand to his forehead, Lang brought it down, wet. The train was not underway. The young man's skin had been agreeably flushed. Perhaps he'd not been referring to the Reichstag, but to the night Lang had blown up the chemical factory, for *Testament*. There had been scores of onlookers, and he'd been introduced to several of them.

Lang put thumb and forefinger to the squeeze latches on each side of the window. With some effort he got the pane to slide down several notches, affording him a clear view of trackside.

Toward the front of the train great billows of steam were emerging from the undercarriage. Caught in the platform lamplight the steam appeared substantive, nearly solid. A peak-capped porter with three suitcases walked toward the cloud and was gone. Another railway employee with some kind of ticket or manifest book was coming toward Lang. For a brief moment the man cast a long, opaque silhouette. Then a drift of condensation came up and the man was engulfed. He did not, as far as Lang could see, reappear. There were many indistinct flickerings, as of gauzy draperies when the wind is blowing, or of cigarette smoke in the beam of a film projector, as the movie cuts from one shot to the next. A cloud of steam, impossibly large, bulged toward him, dense, ominous, black, edges aglow with an eerie fluorescence.

He'd not eaten to speak of since the night before, and was just now beginning to feel the hunger. He would feign sleep until the border—Lang knew from previous trips that the customs men were inclined to be cursory if you seemed wealthy and not in a mood to be disturbed. Once across, he'd go to the dining car, order a martini, perhaps a lean veal chop. After coffee, cognac, he could reclaim the folded sheaf of bills from their cunning niche behind the refund-slip box. All he'd have to remember, really, was to pass up desserts, and to take care not to fill up on bread.

There was a draft of clean cooling air from the open window top. He felt his face tingle where he'd been sweating, and exhaled. They would never let the train depart with himself aboard. Even now Bott must be waiting at the foot of the platform, as Wieland advanced on the Pullman. Wieland would urge him to be sensible: let the innocent passengers depart for Paris, points west, without additional delay. He would appeal to Lang's noblesse oblige. Surely Lang would understand, that there was no further point? Lang would step off the Pullman. The milling crowd would applaud, parting before him as he walked down the platform, Wieland a discreet step behind. Bott would be waiting, joined now by the man from the Ministry.

The roll of adhesive tape was digging into his thigh. He lit a cigarette, his first since he'd boarded.

There was a deep rumbling shudder, which Lang felt in his bowels; and outside the window much exhalation of steam. As the condensation dispersed Lang watched the train across the platform move slowly forward. He was, for a moment, completely lost. Another shudder. An unending perilous instant without movement or sound. Then, with some initial lurching, the platform began to move backward. The scream of metal on metal, as those wheels not yet in revolution were dragged along the rails. A bell clanged, lowering pitch just perceptibly. He could feel it now.

His wife's face, framed by the top of the window. She was walking just quickly enough to keep pace with the train.

"I wanted to say good-bye," she told him.

Her face was momentarily abstracted by a gust of steam. He noticed the small beads of condensation which had formed on the outside of the window, clearing tracks on the dusty surface as they dipped downward.

Lang said, "Thea." Her head bobbed in the window frame as she increased her pace to keep up.

"You should have said something." Her hair glowed, lit from behind by jazzy trackside light.

"Yes," he said, at once quite miserable. He put out the Boyard in the armrest ashtray without taking his eyes from Thea's face. The exhilaration he'd felt, as the train began to move, gone now. Then he heard himself say, "I will always love you." His voice had come out hearty, charming, not at all as he'd intended it.

"I made sure," Thea said, "that there was no one following." The track bed seemed to be inclining upward, for now only the top half of her face showed over the metal sash bar. Her mouth was lost to dust and condensation. Then the track bed dipped and he could make out, once more, her face entire.

She was pushing a small parcel through the opening. It was tied around each edge with thin patisserie string. She said, "You forgot," as he took the manuscript from her. The tip of his fourth finger touched her glove for the least instant. He remembered the keys, the note, the missing pre-Columbian figure. It would not have been difficult for her to figure out what had happened.

"Why," he said finally.

"Why?"

He could not tell from her inflection what she wished to convey. She'd not said "Stay," or "Come back," or let on in any way that she meant to stop him.

"I love you," he said, liking his voice better this time. He hoped she'd not take it as an answer to her question, because it made no sense that way.

Thea missed a step and was abruptly gone. Perhaps three seconds later she reappeared in the window, short of breath. At some point the train would accelerate past her ability to keep up; or the platform would run out. He could not hear her steps for the low throbbing of great machinery. Somewhere behind them the bell had begun to clang. Then Thea said, "Good-bye," and stopped walking.

He put his head fully outside the window She was not more than a meter away. He saw her eyes, her head, her body as she receded. He could no longer clearly make out her features as she turned away from him and began to walk back toward the station.

"Thea."

It was doubtful she'd hear him at this distance, with this noise.

Finally he withdrew and, feeling chilled, made to close the window. He banged repeatedly upward with the heel of his hand. The thing seemed to have gotten wedged, one side higher than the other. He chopped down on the tilted sash bar, sending an acute pain up his wrist and forearm.

The train was out of the station, lowering now into the railyard defile. He felt the weight of the entire train bearing him forward with a fierce momentum, and listened to the clacking of wheels over rail joins, quite rhythmic now. There was a sharp extended whistle which seemed, for some reason, to make the hurt in his forearm worse; and then a Doppler-shifted bell, somewhere trackside.

He held the *Fiaker* manuscript to his forehead. There was something, he noticed now, beneath it, bound in black calf. It was the current volume of his diary. She had thought to see that he not leave it behind. He suddenly knew with some certainty that he would not see her again in this life. He would go to Paris, Thea would stay. The films they had made together would be seen in a new way which struck him, now, with untellable loss. Then he was in the corridor, walking toward the rear of the train.

Entering the dining car, still dark, he retrieved the folded bills from the rear of the refund-slip box. He was afraid for some reason that the far dining car door would be locked; but it was not, and he went through to the rearmost car.

A set of French doors with slatted blinds opened upon an observation platform. It was just large enough to stand upon, with a low ornate railing. Lang shut the doors carefully behind him.

He watched the tracks play out from behind the carriage, joining, splitting into two, joining once more, in exultant demonstration of a switchman's options. His hair blew forward across his forehead and he brushed it from his eyes. The crossties receded one after another, counting out time, as present became past. Now; and now; and now. There was nothing you could do to stop it. He watched the ties, stroboscopic and somehow comforting, as they became lost to the distance, and the dark.

There were fewer tracks. The lines were branching out, each with its specific destination. Then there was just one set of tracks, the one the train was reeling out behind it. The glow of the train's rear lights, a dense crimson, did not penetrate to where the rails converged. By raising his eyes a bit Lang could feel them, coming together, as he left all behind.

He turned toward the French doors. Out of the yard now it was less well lit, but he could make out the reflection of his face, and behind it the rising pattern of rails and ties against the horizontal grain of the blinds, just behind the glass. He watched his lips as he pronounced the syllables of his entire name. Then, working the handle, he was once more inside the car. Lang walked forward to the Pullman, his own progress added to that of the train, picking up speed now, toward the border.